The Jovian Dilemma

John L. Flynn, Ph.D.

Galactic Books
Owings Mills, Maryland

Galactic Books
Post Office Box 1442
Owings Mills, Maryland 21117-9998

The Jovian Dilemma
By John L. Flynn, Ph.D.

PRINTING HISTORY

Second Edition / September 2019

Acknowledgements: I am humbly indebted to Dr. Carl Sagan, the National Aeronautics and Space Administration, the Planetary Society, Edwin Hubbell and the Hubbell Space Telescope, the Voyager probes, Steven Hawking, and the Jet Propulsion Laboratory at the California Institute of Technology.

Editor: Edmund Dantes
Design & Layout: John L. Flynn
Book Cover Design: John L. Flynn

Library of Congress Cataloging in Publication Data
Flynn, John L. The Jovian Dilemma
1. Science Fiction. I. Scientific Theory - Jupiter and the Big Bang.
II. John L. Flynn--Plots, themes, etc. III. Title.

ISBN: 0-9769400-5-1

PRINTED IN THE UNITED STATES OF AMERICA

For

Carl Sagan,
who first suggested the kind of life forms
that may exist on a gas giant

Prologue

"Thousands of years ago, well before the first astrologers charted the passage of stars, primitive man held up a torch in the darkness and called upon the heavens for answers about his earthly fate and destiny. The ancients believed that powerful gods lived among the twinkling lights and shooting flames of the heavens, and that the right spell or combination of magical chants would be enough to penetrate the darkness and move them to action. Jupiter was thought to be the greatest in the pantheon of powerful and warring deities, for he had defeated the titans and given birth to all of the other gods. But he was a jealous and spiteful god, full of anger and rage. More often than not, he would strike down innocent mortals with his powerful thunderbolts just for sport. In time, man replaced Jupiter and the other gods with his newfound beliefs in science and technology. But as the later years of the twenty-first century brought the epoch to a close, mankind again turned to Jupiter for answers about its future..." the tin voice on the recording echoed in the darkness of space.

After its eighteen-month journey to Jupiter, the *Explorer II* airship was reducing speed as it plunged deeper and deeper into the unfathomable depths of the Jovian maelstrom. For every kilometer of depth, the density of the gas around the small, interplanetary craft doubled, and as the tremendous pressures mounted, the airship began to slow its decent.

Within its pressurized, adamantine steel walls, Scott Glenn and Hiroki Takahashi huddled over their control panels. The two astronauts knew they would never reach the surface of Jupiter; any illusions they may have had about climbing out of their small craft and planting a flag on the surface, like the great explorers before them, were quickly dashed by the reality of physics. Deep below the clouds of the Jupiter, the atmospheric pressure was so much greater than anything found on Earth that they would have been crushed to the size of an atom; even the tiniest of the electrons of hydrogen atoms were squeezed out into forms that were completely alien to them. While the sensors aboard their command module, the *Vigilant*, had long since ruled out any signs of intelligent life on the planet, they had detected the huge concentrations of liquid metallic hydrogen that had made their journey so imperative.

At nearly a billion miles from Earth, the gas giant was a remote, impenetrable world, storm-tossed by weather systems that could have easily swallowed the rest of the inner planets of the Solar System whole. Probes to Jupiter in the early decades of the twenty-first century had revealed a vast ocean of dense gas and floating clouds, with no discernible landmasses, no rivers or lakes, no boundaries at all between the planet's molten core and gaseous atmosphere—a world without a surface. Not a hospitable place, scientists concluded, but the only planet with enough raw resources of liquid metallic hydrogen to rescue Earth and its colonies from the current energy crisis. In small quantities, liquid metallic hydrogen was capable of running a large city on Earth for an entire year. So, even before Glenn and

Takahashi had blasted off on their historic journey, energy futures soared on the global stock exchange. Executives of the three major energy corporations envisioned great balloon colonies permanently floating in the Jovian atmosphere, mining its precious energy resources, and quickly consolidated their mutual resources into a plan that would guarantee them a monopoly for decades to come.

The *Explorer II* skirted around the dark rim of a giant whirlpool and continued descending through the huge billowing clouds of methane, ammonia and assorted hydrocarbons, which had formed a canyon larger than the greatest canyons on Earth. Cradled deep within the canyons, the airship was little more than a speck of dust as it raced through the clouds. It was not a sleek craft like so many generations of science fiction artists had depicted in their flights of fancy, but it was very functional. Apart from the huge balloon that spanned over two hundred and fifty feet across and towered a staggering four hundred feet above it, the *Explorer II* airship was surprisingly small and compact. From the heat shield to the network of thick, steel cables that connected the gondola to the balloon above, it was less than twenty meters in length; it was hard to believe that so modest a vehicle, as small as the original *Apollo* space module, could carry two men and tons of excavating equipment.

Scott Glenn and Hiroki Takahashi piloted their small craft with pushbuttons and keystrokes instead of steering wheels and foot breaks. The cabin was extremely cramped, not unlike the interiors of the early *Mercury* and *Gemini* space capsules, and the two astronauts did not have much room to move around. A series of monitors and graphic display screens provided the only illumination in the craft, casting a flickering glow on the faces of the two men. The images on some of the computer displays were constantly changing. One of the screens displayed a three-dimensional image of Jupiter. Another showed the airship and its relative position to the surface of the gas giant. Two other television monitors flickered to life with other key pieces of data. Neither astronaut reacted to the new information. Instead Glenn sat forward in his seat, dictating words into his computer station.

"...for science could provide no more certainty about man's fate or his place in the cosmos than those ancient beliefs of his ancestors," he spoke and then, after a short pause to consider the right turn of phrase, continued, "So, today, on this first historic mission to Jupiter, we still carry the torch of primitive man. But instead of uttering words like abracadabra to rouse the gods to action or sending the cold, unfeeling machines of our technology, we rely on the courage and curiosity and humanity of modern man to penetrate the darkness. We search for answers to those truly profound questions about mankind in the dark depths of the great gas giant."

Takahashi punched the OFF button on one of the displays and leaned back in his seat to consider his co-pilot. They met each other for the first time at the Naval Academy in Annapolis, Maryland, and had spent their first three years as midshipmen fighting to be the best in their class. He was inspired by Glenn's intensity, including the deep blue eyes that seemed to burn right through lesser individuals. Glenn's parents had named him after two of the original *Mercury 7* astronauts, and he was expected to be the epitome of the "right stuff." So, it came as no surprise to him when Glenn, upon graduation, applied to the United States Space Academy and was readily accepted. Hiroki Takahashi, the product of two very different cultures (one American and one Japanese), had no real desire to become an astronaut, but got swept up in Glenn's enthusiasm and fierce competitiveness, and soon followed him into space. The two had been co-pilots ever since, and he would not have had it any other way.

"Glenn, that's the third time in the last hour that you've rewritten the opening of your memoirs," he said, at last.

Scott Glenn flashed a toothy grin. "What else is there to do on this long descent?"

"Sleep," Takahashi replied.

"Not with the way you snore."

"Beats listening to you yammer on hour after hour."

Glenn stared at Takahashi as the clicking sounds of computer relays processing information filled the silent void. The colors, flickering on their faces from the monitors and graphic display screens, cycled gradually from red to orange to white and then back again. Finally, Glenn turned back to his station and his memoirs.

"You know people don't read e-books anymore," Takahashi tried to reason with him. "Now, it's all about virtual simulations and holographic memory implants."

"They'll read this one."

"What makes you so sure?"

Glenn thought for a moment.

"You and I will be celebrities. We'll be the first men in the history of space flight to penetrate the atmosphere of Jupiter," he replied, pumping up his chest with pride. "That's an accomplishment that will go down in the record books, just like Neal Armstrong's giant leap on the moon and Tatiana Rudenko's first steps on Mars."

Hiroki Takahashi had a faraway look in his eyes, which Glenn mistook as a shared vision of fame and glory.

"We'll be famous, my friend," he added, reaching over and patting Takahashi on the back several times with the palm of his hand. "And people just love to read e-books by celebrities, especially famous astronauts like you and me."

Takahashi swallowed deeply. "I just hope we get back in one piece."

After a moment of reflection, it dawned on Glenn that his co-pilot didn't share the same dream, and he scrambled to say something solicitous.

"Thinking about your wife again?"

"Yeah," he replied. "She didn't want me to go on this mission. Said she had some kind of premonition that I wasn't coming back."

"Must be tough being a newlywed," Glenn added.

"What would you know about it?"

"Not a damn thing, Hiroki."

"I promised my wife if I got back in one piece," he confessed, "I was going to settle down and start that family she wants."

Glenn patted him on the back again.

"All right!" he exclaimed, with a cheerful glee in his eyes. "So, when we get back to Earth, I'll publish my memoirs, you'll make lots of babies and we'll both be famous."

"Now that's a plan."

They began a long slow laugh that built until they were laughing with great zest and gusto, but their laughter was cut short by the sound of klaxons.

Glenn's eyes darted from one screen to the other, then fixed on one in front of him, on the center console.

"The proximity alarm!" he shouted.

He punched in several commands on his keyboard and struck the ENTER key. The television monitor flickered to life. Next to it, on the graphic display, the airship shrunk in size until it was not much more than a dot.

"The sensors did a full sweep of this area," Takahashi reported. "There were no land masses, mountain ridges, or obstructions of any kind. There's not supposed to be anything for ten thousand kilometers."

"I know...I know. Nothing but hot air."

Glenn was studying the graphic display. He glanced at the television monitor for an instant, then turned back. Suddenly, on the central display, the dot that represented the *Explorer II* was surrounded by thousands of other dots.

"Jesus Christ!" Glenn exclaimed.

Takahashi leaned over to view the display. His head was almost by Glenn's ear as both of them were transfixed by what they saw. Speechless, they turned together and gaped at the television monitor on the left. Once the exterior camera had completed a full pass, it began panning a second time.

For a fraction of a second, a dark shape slid by the bottom of the screen. Glenn instantly pushed the key that controlled the panning motion of the camera and reversed the pan to get another look. The dark shape reappeared on the bottom of the screen and caused both of them to jerk back from the monitor at the same time.

"What the Hell is that?" Glenn said, startled. He quickly pushed the tilt keys and the shape rose in the screen. On the television monitor, the shape was obviously very large, but did not have any distinctive features or markings. It was still a bit too far away to get any clear detail.

"Is it chemical? Organic?" Takahashi asked.

Glenn punched several commands into his keyboard. The television image shook for a moment, then, as the depth of field in the monitor started to change, the dark shape began growing larger. At first, it was blurry, but as the zoom on the camera lens slowly moved toward it, the image came into focus. For an instant, several clouds floated by and obscured the image. But as the camera lens pushed through the clouds, a huge, lumbering hunk of protoplasm appeared.

It was but one of several thousand that filled the sky. Some looked like giant balloons that expanded and contracted at will; others were formless like the simple amoeba, and still others appeared long and cigar-like. They seemed to have no distinctive features, like eyes or ears or mouths. Their physical structure or torso, if that was the proper term, had no distinguishing marks or blemishes, and they very nearly blended into the background of their surroundings. Gathered together in a great lazy herd that stretched for thousands of miles, certainly further than the eye of the camera could see, these Jovian lifeforms were larger than the greatest whales that ever lived on Earth. They seemed peaceful and benevolent, floating in the clouds and grazing like cattle on the tiniest of organic molecules.

On the central display monitor, the *Explorer II* looked like a dinghy in an ocean of supertankers, but Glenn and Takahashi could not tear themselves away from the live feed on the television screen.

"They don't appear to be hostile," Takahashi commented.

"How can you tell?" Glenn asked, his eyes as big as saucers.

"Well, they haven't tried to eat us yet."

"I don't think we should wait around to find out."

"We've got to report this to the *Vigilant*."

"Yeah," Glenn replied, with his jaw hanging open. "Only, I'm not sure exactly what to report."

All of a sudden, a blinding flash caught them by surprise.

A burst of lightning, in actuality the mother of all electrostatic discharges, blasted through the hull of the airship, and all the interior lights exploded into a shower of sparks. The television monitor and all other graphic displays blanked milk white with a dark burn in the center. Then they were black. The screens flashed white for a fraction of a second, then were black again. Takahashi was frozen in place, while Glenn rubbed his eyes and stared back at the dead monitor. Both men had seen something, but neither knew what to make of it. Suddenly, the reality of their situation caught up to them, and both began frantically flicking buttons.

"Systems are out all over the ship," he said, in panic.

"I've got no power and we're losing pressure fast," Takahashi reported.

"Try the manual restart."

"That'll take ten minutes."

"We don't have ten minutes," Glenn cried, recalling his first year physics. "If we don't get that pressure equalized in the next couple of minutes, the outside atmosphere will crush this ship to the size of a tin can."

"I always wondered what it would be like to be a sardine."

"Well, I'd rather not find out."

"What about the balloon's manual release valve?" Takahashi asked, thinking quickly. "Couldn't we flush its gases right into the cockpit."

"Yeah, but we'd also increase our speed of descent."

"You got a better idea."

Glenn shook his head. "Damned if we do. Damned if we don't."

Takahashi reached up over his head and started to crank a large, round valve to the right. It was difficult work, and the more he struggled with it, the less he was able to budge it. Glenn reached up with both hands and added his strength to Takahashi's actions. The two men struggled with all of their might to open the valve.

Takahashi said, through gritted teeth, "Just think, this'll make a great chapter in your book."

"That is, if we make it—"

Just then, the two astronauts heard a loud, horrible, metallic sound, like a tin can being crushed between the mighty jaws of a great white shark, and they turned to stare at the interior hull. One section of the airship's thick, adamantine steel hull crumpled inward, like a piece of aluminum foil yielding in the palm of someone's hand. Then another section crumpled.

Glenn's jaw sagged as he looked at the hull. "Oh, my God," he shouted, but never heard the words.

The hull finally collapsed inward.

Glenn and Takahashi did not have time to react; after all, there was probably very little that they could have done had they reacted in time. Within that nanosecond between heartbeats, the hull of the airship folded in upon itself, then exploded outward in a brilliant flash that lit up the sky with fireworks.

Emerging from the canyon of clouds, the gondola of the airship was blown away from its towering balloon and tumbled end over end, like a football kicked for a field goal, breaking into millions of pieces as it fell. The large balloon, now severed from its lower half, floated pointlessly through the atmosphere, gradually losing gas and descending into the clouds below. In a matter of seconds, there was no trace of the *Explorer II* airship, no trace of the two brave astronauts, no trace of anything. All evidence had been swept clean by the Jovian winds.

Several hours later, the Captain of the *Vigilant* was forced to abandon all attempts at a rescue operation. He reported to Earth that the crew of the *Explorer II* was missing, presumed dead.

Monday

1

Mesmerized, Mitchell Ryan stared out the small porthole of the *Montgolfier* as the Great Red Spot of Jupiter began to swallow his fragile craft whole. The great column of gas reached high above the adjacent clouds, and reduced his airship to a tiny, insignificant speck in an area large enough to contain half a dozen Earths. At over a million years old, the gigantic storm system afforded him a rare glimpse into the inferno that must have once given birth to moons, planets, stars and whole galaxies. Somewhere behind him, he knew an orbiting space station and the faint flicker of light that was home were receding into the vast obscurity of space.

The *Montgolfier* airship was a second-generation, high-atmosphere bathyscaphe which bore only a superficial resemblance to the *Explorer II*. Like its predecessor, the airship was made up of a large balloon and a small gondola. The balloon spanned nearly double the volume of the other, measuring over 400 feet across and towering 700 feet above its lower half. It was not fully inflated and appeared to be losing volume as it descended toward Jupiter. The gondola, also larger in size than the *Explorer II*, was a jumble of Mylar, camera and radar equipment, solar panels, and a flat, inches-thick Plexiglas porthole. It was suspended beneath the balloon by a network of thick, adamantine-steel cables.

"No other view like it in the entire solar system," the Pilot remarked.

Ryan turned from the porthole and grunted. His face was as pale as a white linen shroud. He tried to mask his fear behind the comfortable and finely tailored Saville Row suit and striped tie, but his fifty-year-old good looks and elegant grooming could not hide the fact that he was scared shitless. He hadn't always been afraid. Back on Earth, he had been known as a man of formidable power and influence. He had served two terms of office in the Senate and three terms in the House of Representatives with distinction, fighting for many conservative platforms. His shining moment came during the height of the rebellion on Mars when he argued against secession and cast the deciding vote that prevented the colonies from joining other non-aligned worlds. Of course, that vote had lead to a bloody, four-year civil war with Mars, and subsequently triggered the terrorist attacks that were now all too common throughout the Solar System. But Ryan never backed down from his position, and that unwavering devotion meant a great deal to his constituency and the Republican party. When the cabinet-level post to the Jupiter colony became vacant, only the name of one man was recommended to the President as a replacement, and that name was Mitchell Ryan.

Ryan never imagined, in his wildest imaginings, the sense of devastating fear that he felt looking out the porthole of the small airship. His hands tenaciously gripped the armrests of his seat and his well-manicured fingernails dug deeply into the expensive Corinthian leather upholstery.

"You know, we're not actually going down into the Eye," the Pilot added. She flicked several switches to bring the craft around, then stretched to point to a spot on the horizon. "We're descending to that blue area just to the right, but we use the air currents and updrafts from the Eye to slow our descent." She leaned in closer. "You wouldn't think so—what with that raging motherfucker of a storm below us—but there's actually much less turbulence than if we had descended over one of the bands. Besides, this way we also avoid the clouds that are composed mainly of ammonia crystals."

She then slid back into her seat and fingered several buttons that caused the craft to shudder like an elevator that had slipped between floors.

"What the hell's going on?" Ryan demanded, as he felt the bile of his stomach suddenly in his throat.

"Just routine, Mister. Ryan." Her voice was firm and confident. "Nothing to worry about."

"Why are we suddenly slowing?"

"We have to cycle over to another mixture while the cabin adjusts to the ambient pressure," she responded. She adjusted several controls above her head and Ryan felt a hiss sound pierce his inner eardrums. "We used to pressurize the ship entirely with helium, but people kept complaining about how cold it got and how it made their voices sound like Squeaky Mouse." The hissing sound gradually dissipated. "So, now we use a rather exotic mixture of gases."

Sliding out of his seat, Ryan squeezed next to the Pilot for a better look at the instruments. They were covered with moisture and she had to keep rubbing the condensation away from the video display terminals with a cloth rag in order to read the incoming data.

Ryan felt very cold. He blew into his cupped hands, then rubbed his arms up and down with the palms of his hands to keep warm.

"And how does this pressurization affect the oxygen we breathe?" he asked.

"We don't breathe oxygen down here."

"Why not?"

"For the same reason you don't breathe it on the eighteen-month trip from Earth," she answered with a sigh. "Pure oxygen under pressure is pretty toxic, and at the depths we're descending, breathing the twenty-one or so percent oxygen you're used to on the Station is like taking a shower with hydrochloric acid. You'd burn the insides of your lungs right out."

"So, what are we supposed to breathe then?"

"Down here, you breathe about two percent oxygen and ninety-eight percent other gases," she replied.

Ryan stared off into space.

After a moment of thought, he spoke again. "I suppose that's what the miners, engineers and other members of my team will be breathing when they're aboard the mining platform?"

"You can't exist down here without it."

Ryan gulped down a deep breath. "Any risks to long term exposure?"

"Well, the first surveyors complained of extreme headaches, dizziness and hallucinations, but none of them lived long enough to have our medical staff run a full diagnostic."

"Yes, I read about that in the report," he replied. "But I also seem to remember something about one or more of them claiming they saw ghosts of the first expedition team that was lost here."

The Pilot grinned at him over her shoulder and said, without emotion, "You spend enough time in hostile environments like this one, Mister Ryan, and you'll imagine seeing just about anything."

"Do you believe in ghosts?"

"Ghosts? Yeah, sure, who doesn't?" she responded. "But it wasn't ghosts that killed those men."

"Killed?" Ryan caught a glimpse of apprehension in her face before she turned away from him and back to her controls. "But the report concluded that they had all died of long-term exposure."

"They may have breathed in the wrong mixture of gases, but that isn't what killed them," she said. She punched another set of routine commands into her keyboard, then flicked another switch overhead. "I've seen men die of nitrogen narcosis and oxygen toxemia; it's not a pretty site watching friends vomit up what's left of their lungs because all of the tissue's been burned away. I've also watched others with high pressure nervous syndrome put a bullet in their head or flush themselves out an airlock rather than let their brains turn into Jell-O."

Ryan shook his head in silence. He had to admit to himself that he had not fully considered any, or all, of these factors when he agreed to take over the project. He had never even considered the human factor. Issues related to occupational safety, health and workman's compensation had completely eluded him.

"But those surveyors didn't die or commit suicide," she concluded. "Their minds were literally ripped out of their heads by something that we've never before encountered out here."

"The Jovians?"

"You said it, Mister Ryan, not me."

"Then you don't believe the rumors about the discovery some new lifeform?"

"No," she said flatly, punching another set of buttons on her console, "and I don't believe in flying saucers or little green men either."

Without warning, the *Montgolfier* rolled to one side, then plummeted down like a falling elevator out of control.

"What the—!" he exclaimed, falling back into his passenger seat, the words shaking out of his mouth. Ryan found himself sinking deeper and deeper into the cushions the more he tried to right himself.

"We've completed our initial pressurization and are now headed down," she reported, hunching over the telemetry console. "We still have to make a couple of adjustments before we reach the Platform, but I figure we'll be there in less than twenty minutes or so."

The series of monitors and graphic display screens illuminated her face with a flickering glow of data. She shot him a glance over her shoulder. "Just try to sit back and enjoy the ride."

2

The huge billowing clouds of the Jovian atmosphere parted to reveal the *Montgolfier* as it neared its destination, the Mining Platform. Both the airship and the platform were dwarfed by the soft, pink gaseous clouds; in fact, the Mining Platform bobbed in and out of the cloud surface, like a small dinghy alone and adrift in a great ocean, as the airship made its final approach. The platform appeared fairly primitive by Earth standards, just a collection of tin cans, a couple of solar panels and a long, narrow coil that stretched from the central core down into the vast reaches of the planet, but was supposed to be the latest in modular design. Ryan had hoped to make a visual inspection, but he could barely move in his seat.

"Just relax," the Pilot said, hovering anxiously above him. "Try to keep your eyes closed and your mind focused on something else."

Ryan's face had turned from pale to ashen by the time they reached the Mining Platform deep within the atmosphere of Jupiter. The queasy sensation he had felt earlier was threatening to explode all over the pressurized cabin of the *Montgolfier*. But he somehow managed to contain the feeling of space sickness by digging his fingernails deeply into the armrests of his seat, his knuckles turning white. He closed his eyes tightly, and tried to imagine that he was somewhere else.

The *Montgolfier* pilot placed an oxygen mask over his face. "Now breathe deeply," she commanded.

Ryan took a deep breath, but then coughed into the mask. He felt like such a baby being mothered by this attractive woman who was young enough to be his daughter, yet still old enough to be certified shuttle pilot.

"Again…"

Ryan took another breath and seemed to breathe easier.

"That's good. How do you feel? " she asked, removing the mask just long enough for him to respond to her question.

"Just like I did after I took my first smoke."

The *Montgolfier* Pilot smiled pleasantly and straightened up. "Just relax, Mister Ryan. Take a couple more deep breaths and try to remain calm. The feeling of nausea should pass shortly."

Ryan took a gulp of air. His breathing was deep and erratic compared to the steady, soft sound of her respiration.

"Are we there yet?" he mumbled through the mask.

"I was just starting our final approach."

"Can I open my eyes?"

"Yes," she replied, "but try not to move your head too quickly and look around the cabin."

Ryan opened his eyes and saw her face staring down at him. He struggled to sit up in his seat, but failed. He still had not mastered the trick of moving in freefall and was disappointed with himself that he needed her help to move. Like a caretaker with a wheel-chair bound senior, she put her hand behind his back and helped him sit up straight. He acknowledged her assistance with a nod of gratitude, and gulped down a few more hits of oxygen.

"I can't wait to get my feet back on solid ground," he sighed.

"Solid ground," she laughed, moving back to her command seat. "That's about a billion miles in the other direction."

"You know what I mean."

She nodded. "Just relax. We'll be there in a few minutes." Ryan settled back in his seat, adjusting the safety harness around his waist and shoulders. He placed the small bottle of oxygen and oxygen mask in the folds of the cushion on his right side, within careful reach. His hands then gripped the armrests as he leaned back to study the monitor overhead. The graphical interface displayed a dot that represented the airship closing on the dot that represented the Mining Platform, and at long last, he felt a sense of comfort and relief.

"Mister Ryan, may I ask you a question?"

"Certainly," he answered, watching her execute a handful of expert maneuvers on the command console from his back seat.

"You're a civilian," she said, measuring her words carefully, "and a mature man in his fifties. From the finely tailored suit you are wearing to the manicure and the way you carry yourself, you are obviously a man of great taste and elegance. Just what the hell are you doing all the way out here?"

"Don't tell me you're one of those cultural separatists who think that deep space exploration should be reserved for the young?"

"No, not at all," she replied. "It's just that this is not exactly a tourist spot. We're in the middle of a war zone here, and there's no telling when those terrorist factions on Mars will strike again. And then, there's all those strange, unexplained things that keep happening."

"I see no real cause for alarm," Ryan said calmly. "The fleet has implemented a blockade of all ships going in and out of Mars, and our own Station's defenses are all at heightened state of alert. We're probably safer in Jovian space than on any other colony in the solar system."

"No offense, sir, but you just don't know the situation here."

"Well, Lieutenant. That's why I'm here. To learn."

The Pilot looked up from her control panel, but only for an instant. The sound of metal clanging against metal and the sharp jolt of mass reacting against mass gave them both a start. With a thud, the *Montgolfier* and the Mining Platform made contact. The massive pads, located just inside the mining platform's docking ring, clamped onto the section directly below the airship's round command module. Then the hydraulic pads on the docking ring tightened over the escape hatch, locking the airship into place, like a baby riding piggyback on its mother.

"Docking complete," she reported into her headset.

A few seconds later, they heard metallic, scratching noises from outside the hatch, then a loud hissing sound of air as the pressures equalized. Finally, the airlock opened, and a man wearing lightweight knit slacks and a short-sleeved shirt, which was almost the uniform of the Station personnel, climbed into the cabin. He was a strong, hulking man who looked thirty-five, but was actually twenty years older. He looked like a person who had spent most of his adult life in the gym, lifting weights and riding motionless bicycles, but that was only half true. He had also spent four years at the University of Toronto, earning a degree in criminal justice, and three years of law school at Cambridge.

"Pleased to meet you, Mister Ryan. I'm Lloyd Cramden, your Chief of Security. I came down on the ship before yours to make certain everything was secure for your visit. Doctor Takahashi will be meeting us shortly in the airlock."

They shook hands; then Ryan smiled at the Pilot and said, "Thanks for an informative ride. Perhaps I'll see you on the way back."

The *Montgolfier* Pilot nodded, then turned back to her control panel.

3

Ryan looked down through the hatch. He saw a bank of red lights below, which he rightly assumed was the warning signal that the outer hatch was open. He watched as Cramden climbed through it, took hold of a ladder and began descending to the next deck headfirst. Weightless, he hauled himself, hand over hand through the airlock hatch, and took hold of the ladder with his right hand. Above his head, the hatch snapped shut and he watched the wheel spin closed. He heard a clank as the bathyscaphe unhitched, then the sound of its engines as it headed back to the Station. Finally, the bank of lights over his head flashed from red to yellow.

Ryan followed Cramden down the ladder, feeling the weight of gravity take gradual hold of him. At first, his weight was so slight that he had almost to force himself downward by using the rungs of the ladder as a handhold. Not until he reached the middle rung, had he acquired enough weight to swing himself around and continue climbing down the ladder feet first. When he stepped off the final rung onto the metal deck, his feet were at last on solid ground, and he reacted to this knowledge by firmly stomping his right foot on the deck several times. Cramden smiled, as the foot stomps echoed through the airlock and into the large circular chamber beyond.

"Feels good to get your feet back on solid ground, doesn't it?" the Security Chief commented aloud.

"More than you can know," Ryan said.

"I've been here for four years now and I still haven't gotten used to that whole business of weightlessness."

"That doesn't sound very encouraging, Chief."

Cramden checked his chronometer, then looked around the airlock. "Can I get you anything while we're waiting for Doctor Takahashi?" he asked, pointing at one of the vending machines. "She should be here at any moment."

"I could really use a cup of black coffee, with two lumps."

"Right, Mister Ryan...I'll see what I can do. Coffee is in somewhat short supply lately with the blockade around Mars, and I haven't seen a lump of sugar in more than eighteen months."

"I'd settle for a cup of hot water right about now," Ryan added.

"Well, I think we can do better than hot water," Cramden sighed, turning to one of the vending machines.

Just then, the comlink on his belt chimed. "I'm sorry, Mister Ryan. I've got to take this. Perhaps you'd be more comfortable in the departure lounge? It's just through there."

Ryan nodded and took a few steps away, acknowledging his Security Chief's desire to respond to the communication in private. He walked out of the airlock and into the darkness of the large circular chamber that was just beyond. Instantly, the recessed lighting sparkled to life and revealed a plain but comfortable lounge. Besides the usual chairs, small tables, sofas and loveseats, there was a billiard table, several old-fashioned pinball tables, television monitors, computers and pictophones. The walls were decorated with photographs and posters of exotic locales on Earth, not unlike the departure lounge at any major spaceport in the system.

"Senator Ryan," a soft voice called to him from the shadows, "I hope your trip down here was a pleasant one?"

Ryan looked momentarily startled, but turned to greet her with a firm handshake, which she returned in kind. The Japanese scientist was short, very petite, with a nondescript figure, and two, piercing brown eyes. Her porcelain-like features were cool, composed, even somewhat detached. She was dressed very simply in casual work clothes, tennis shoes and a white smock. She wore the identification badge on her smock like the badge of a sheriff in a frontier town.

"I'm afraid to admit that I'm not a very good passenger, Doctor Takahashi," he replied, with a warm smile.

"Your pilot signaled ahead, and said that you had taken suddenly ill," she said as a matter of fact. "Are you all right now?"

"Yes, thank you."

"We have all experienced similar discomforts on our first trip down."

"If only I could have been frozen, Doctor…"

The Security Officer had now approached and was standing at a respectful distance holding a Styrofoam cup in his hands. Cramden waited for a natural pause in the conversation, then interjected, "Well, I see you two have already met. Would you like something to drink, Doctor Takahashi?"

"No, thank you."

Ryan took a drink from his cup and smiled. The flavor of the Earl Grey tea was an acceptable substitute to coffee for his pallet, but more importantly it warmed his cold insides. For the moment, while he drank down several gulps of his tea, Ryan exchanged awkward glances with Cramden and the Japanese scientist, then realized that they were both waiting for him to complete the rest of his thought.

"I was just explaining that, on my journey here from Earth, I opted for the deep freeze after that grueling slingshot around Mars," he continued, looking politely from one person to the other. "There was no way I was going to let them bounce me through the asteroid belt or put me through aerobraking around Jupiter unless I was fully sedated or frozen in nitrogen gas."

Cramden laughed. "I got shit-faced drunk the first time I came out here."

Takahashi raised an eyebrow on the word "drunk," but tried very hard not to reveal her disapproval. "And how did the members of your family fair on the trip, Senator?"

Ryan took another drink of his tea.

"My two boys and their mother are still back on Earth," he said at last.

"What a pity that you are so very far from home and the ones you love."

"We felt it was best for them," he explained. "Tom's a senior and captain of the football team at Penn State, and Bill's in his first year at Maryland. I didn't see any reason to disrupt their school schedule just to bring them here with me."

"And your wife?" she asked.

"My wife and I have been separated for three years now, Doctor."

"That is most unfortunate."

"Yes, very unfortunate," Ryan responded sadly, "but I don't really blame her. She gave me two fine sons and twenty-five wonderful years of marriage. She's actually a pretty incredible woman and deserves so much better than this."

"Oh?" Cramden said.

Ryan drank down the rest of his tea, crumpled the Styrofoam cup in his hand and tossed it in a nearby waste bin.

"When the war broke out, she wanted me to take a safe job with the diplomatic corps back on Earth, but I knew I could do so much more out here," he said, devoid of any emotion or expression. "I guess she would have come if I had asked her, but by then, things were so hectic that it was better for her to stay behind in Baltimore and start a whole new life for herself."

The sound of recycled air flowing through the ventilation ducts overhead filled the void of silence as the three professionals shifted their weight uneasily and looked at each other with blank faces. The welcome chime of the Security Chief's comlink broke the awkward silence.

Cramden reacted to his comlink. "I'm afraid that I am going to have to take care of this myself," he reported. "I'll try to catch up to the two of you later in the forward observation chamber."

Ryan nodded at Cramden, then looked at Takahashi. She smiled slightly at the gentleman's visible discomfort at being left alone with her, then turned with little movement and started down the corridor. Ryan followed.

"Are your family members with you on the Station, Doctor?" he asked.

"My five year-old son Hiroshi and his paternal grandmother live with me on the Station," she replied, no more, no less.

"Son? I wasn't aware that you had a son."

"Yes, he is all that remains of my husband's legacy."

Ryan's face twisted into a knot.

"Your husband is well remembered as a great explorer who died on the first Jupiter probe," he stammered. "But that was fifteen years ago? Right?"

"He was reported missing fifteen years ago," she corrected him, "but his death was never confirmed."

"I'm sorry. I didn't mean to sound so insensitive," he said, measuring his words carefully. "I guess I'm just a little surprised that you and your husband had a five year-old son."

Takahashi continued walking down the corridor, away from departure lounge.

"My son reminds me everyday, perhaps not in words, but in the way he looks at me with his father's eyes, that the work I am doing here is for him and the generations that follow him, and not for me alone."

Ryan followed behind her. "Yes, of course, the success of this mining operation is tremendously important for our children and the future of our planet."

"And yet there are other children whose silent voices cry out to be heard," she said, without any emotion or intonation, "but their cries are not being heeded, are they, Senator Ryan?"

Ryan sighed. He felt like a grandmaster chess player had just expertly maneuvered him into a fool's mate. "Doctor, I read your preliminary report to the United Planets over two years ago and I've yet to see a single shred of evidence that proves those…," he struggled for the right word, "…things out there, whatever you call them, are living, sentient beings. Most of your fellow scientists back on Earth are convinced they're little more than bacteria feeding like parasites on the precious minerals that we've come here to mine."

"I've been observing the Jovian lifeforms for nearly three and a half years now, and their behavior suggests a higher level of consciousness."

"I'm not interested in fantasy, Doctor, just cold, hard facts that are thoroughly grounded in science. Show me your proof and I'll support whatever recommendation you make to the U.P."

Ryan and Takahashi passed through a sliding glass partition into another corridor and followed the narrow passageway around a corner. The glass partition automatically closed behind them. They walked by a series of storage compartments which contained the instruments and equipment needed for the actual excavating process, built right into the bulkhead of the mining platform. Further along, they passed a series of smaller crew compartments, which housed the cooking, washing, living and toilet facilities of the miners that would be reporting for work in a few days. Each cubicle had its own data and telemetry monitors, and was lighted overhead with recessed fluorescent lights. Even though the narrow corridors were illuminated, Ryan felt they were still dark, ominous and claustrophobic. He imagined that a person could get swallowed up by the darkness and never be heard from again.

They continued walking in silence for a few moments; then finally Ryan spoke. "If these 'Jovians' are sentient, then why haven't they contacted us all these years? We've been sending probes to Jupiter for more than a century. In fact, your husband was part of a routine planetary survey, but he never reported making contact with any kind of sentient beings."

"Perhaps he never had the opportunity to file a report."

Ryan shook his head. "The probability that simple organisms would evolve into complex lifeforms on an inhospitable world like this, and that those complex lifeforms would then, in turn, gain sentience is highly unlikely. I see no evidence of an alien civilization. No cities or other structures. Whatever is down may well be, by your definition, a lifeform; but without something more concrete to go on, I'm afraid the mining operation goes ahead as scheduled."

"In New Japan, we are still raised to respect all life as sacred, from the smallest insect to the largest ocean mammal," she reported.

"Yes, I am aware of your many customs and rituals and I don't have a problem with any of them. I'd actually welcome the chance to negotiate the mining rights to their planet with these creatures, but so far not one of them has come forward to bargain. They're like ants rushing about moving dirt from one place to another."

"Ants do serve a purpose."

"True...but whose?" Ryan asked. "Certainly not their own, since they don't accomplish anything to help themselves. Years and years of evolution and they're still nothing but ants."

"Are human beings any better?"

"I would like to think so. I would like to think that the spark of humanity is a beacon to other space faring civilizations...a torch held up in the cold darkness of space that represents enlightenment and order."

"Well, you are wrong," she said with authority. "Humanity is like a cancer that is spreading throughout this solar system."

Ryan disagreed with her and knew this interchange of views would amount to nothing. "It's a good thing there are practical people like me around," he boasted, trying to turn the discussion around, "otherwise, if we left things in the hands of the scientists, there'd be no progress at all."

"Progress? You call this progress, Senator? We have used

up all of the natural resources of our own world, and now must mine those resources on other worlds. What happens when we have used up all the resources in the solar system? What then? Humanity goes onto the next star and over mines that system as well?"

"That's the fourth time you've called me Senator," he observed. "I resigned my seat in Congress two years ago to take this post."

"I beg your humble pardon. I was mistaken," she replied. "I suppose the title of Governor would be more appropriate."

The former Senator shook his head.

"No, I'm afraid that's not been approved yet either. And until the Jupiter colony is officially recognized as a territory of the United States, you'd better just call me by name. Without a title."

Takahashi stopped walking and turned around to face him head on. Her face was without emotion or expression. She ran a delicate hand through her short black hair, and Ryan noted that was the first involuntary action she had made since his arrival.

The Japanese scientist finally said, "You seem reluctant to discuss the possible ecological threat your strip mining poses to the Jovian lifeforms."

"I refuse to add my voice to those environmental groups who have used terrorism and extortion to shut this project down," he replied. "Besides, you know as well as I do, Doctor, how important these resources are to our families back home. The liquid metallic hydrogen alone, in small quantities, is enough to satisfy the energy requirements of a major city on the Earth for nearly a year. The other gases provide the raw fuel for transportation, commerce, industry and..."

"...war," she interrupted.

"And war!" he exclaimed. "The conflict with the terrorist factions on Mars has depleted most of our natural resources."

"So, we just trade one lifeform for another?"

Ryan shrugged his shoulders.

"I wish there was some other way, but we simply don't have any choice in the matter."

"A matter of this importance surely deserves much more than a footnote in some planetary survey," she returned. "What happens if your mining operation destroys the planet's delicate ecological balance? We must have a contingency plan to preserve some of the natural habitat for the Jovian lifeforms. Otherwise, they may well be faced with extinction."

"Over a century ago, on Earth, certain environmental groups tried to stop loggers in the Pacific Northwest of the United States from cutting down timber in order to save the spotted owl from extinction," Ryan said as he glared at the Japanese scientist. "They chained themselves to trees, blocked roads and destroyed equipment; and when that proved ineffective, they began killing the loggers and the Federal deputies who had been called upon to restore the peace. Their actions not only cost the logging companies millions of dollars in revenue, but also led to the loss of life...all in the name of one endangered species of bird that ultimately disappeared on its own. I'm not going to let that happen here."

All at once, the Mining Platform shuddered and all of the lights and power winked out, but only for an instance. Ryan reacted by flattening himself against the bulkhead, but Takahashi remained calm and cool and collected.

"What the Hell was that!"

"An electrostatic discharge," she answered.

"A what?"

"A stroke of lightning. Perhaps."

"How often does that happen?" he demanded.

"Every couple of days...more or less."

Ryan struggled back to his feet, brushed off his suit and adjusted his tie, trying not to reveal that he was momentarily scarred out of his wits. But she could see right through him.

"You don't think that was a random occurrence, do you?"

"Every lifeform, from the smallest amoeba to the largest mammal of the sea, has its own unique way of communicating," she declared, almost reverently. "Perhaps, just as individual thoughts are sent as electric impulses in the brain, the Jovians use these electrostatic discharges as a way to communicate with each other."

"Right," Ryan snorted his disapproval. He paused for a moment to collect his thoughts, then added, "And you would like nothing more than to hold up the opening of this platform so that you could prove your theory. Maybe get your name in all of the science books."

"I never meant to suggest…"

"The company has agreed to fund your research through the end of the century," he interrupted. "You'll have all the time you need to prove that theory of yours provided you tender a report which is favorable to the operation."

Takahashi was gravely silent. She squeezed her delicate hands into fists hanging down at her sides.

Ryan glanced at his Rolex chronometer, then looked back at her. "My appointment as the Station's Chief Administrator becomes effective on Wednesday at noon. I'll expect your final report no later than Thursday morning. That leaves you just about three days to come up with something more definite on those things of yours for the survey. If the report is not on my desk by Thursday, then I'll expect your resignation in its place. Do I make myself clear?"

Doctor Takahashi nodded that she understood.

"Now, if you don't mind, I'd like to continue my tour of the platform," Ryan said, storming by her in the narrow corridor and purposely nudging her off balance as he passed. "I still haven't seen the forward observation chamber and that was foremost on my agenda today."

4

The forward observation chamber appeared to be a cramped maze of monitors and controls, approximately thirty-five feet across and twenty feet wide, and its interior seemed uncomfortably close to Ryan as he stepped through the only hatch into and out of the chamber. Inside the oblong, double-walled compartment, he tried to imagine what working conditions would be like for the five technicians and three miners he had chosen for the project. The quarters were definitely tight and, as he surveyed the room, he couldn't think of a single item they could do without. Most of the equipment and instruments they would need for the actual drilling and mining process had been built right into the bulkhead. The main instrument panel was a glowing Christmas tree of red and green and yellow lights. Above, there were eight different monitors; one of them had a television image of the view forward, while the images on the other display screens were constantly changing, detailing telemetry, weather conditions and other relevant data. The chamber also contained two toilet facilities, a washroom, a first aid station and a small kitchenette.

As he walked the length and breath of the compartment, acknowledging the three technicians who were on duty with a friendly nod, Ryan was not surprised by the lack of pressure suits or escape pods. The least rupture in the Platform's outer hull would spell instant death. They'd never survive in a suit or have time enough to climb into an escape pod as the outside pressure would crush them instantly. *Thank goodness*, he thought, the likelihood of such an occurrence was extremely rare, what with the Platform's various backup systems and redundancy plans.

The former Senator was next drawn to the chamber's most distinctive feature, a fifteen-foot-wide, ten-foot-high concave window. Constructed of a high-impact Plexiglas, it overlooked the cloudy and sometimes stormy surface of Jupiter. His pulse quickened as he craned forward for a better view.

"So, where are these so-called Jovian lifeforms of yours?" he asked, cupping his hands to the glass and staring out the window.

"I have been scanning the horizon for over an hour, but I can find no sign of them," one of the technicians replied.

"Mister Ryan, this is my assistant, Doctor Masaki Shibata," Takahasi added.

Ryan turned to regard him. Shibata was tall for an Asian male, and his youthful appearance belied his forty-five years—the last ten of which he had spent as Doctor Takahashi's assistant. Presently, he was attending to the various instruments that were measuring data from the atmosphere of Jupiter.

"*Konnichi wa*, Ryan-*san*," he said, first bowing, then shaking hands firmly. "I have been looking forward to meeting you."

"*Konnichi wa*," Ryan returned the greeting with a respectful bow. Then he asked how the scientist was doing, "*Ikaga desu ka?*"

"*Okagasama de genki desu*, Ryan-*san*," he replied warmly, explaining that he was very well. "*Anata wa?*"

"*Hai!*" Ryan affirmed.

"Do you speak Japanese?" Takahashi asked, attempting to mask her surprise at his perfect pronunciation with an innocent question. Her disguise was not entirely effective for Ryan saw right through it.

"No, not really. Only a handful of words and phrases," he responded with a modest shrug. "The product of a misspent youth. I was once a big fan of animaé, and the only way to see the complete uncut versions of those animated movies was in the original Japanese."

"Senator Ryan, I'm Rachel Westin, Chief Science Officer," another technician interjected, thrusting her hand right through an opening in the maze of monitors and controls and taking his right hand in hers.

Startled, Ryan shook her hand and said, "Nice to meet you, Miss Westin."

"Doctor Westin," she corrected.

"Doctor."

"Are you just another suit on a fact-finding tour, or do you actually have some pull with what happens around here?" she asked, abruptly.

"Depends on what you have in mind," he replied.

Ryan walked around the bank of monitors and paused to consider Rachel Westin. He looked at her from head to toe and smiled. She was young, perhaps late thirties or early forties, attractive and smart, with the body of a French fashion model and, according to her personnel file, the intellect of an Einstein. She had been reading the telemetry from an overhead monitor when he entered the chamber, for Ryan had definitely noticed her. To him, she was the most beautiful thing he had seen in the eighteen months since he left Earth.

"We have a rare opportunity here to study a completely different form of life," Westin insisted, with all of the enthusiasm and passion of a first-year student at a graduate seminar at Princeton or Yale.

The former Senator groaned, "So I've been told."

"All that we've ever known about life in the universe has been based on studying life on our own planet. But the simple, undeniable fact remains that every living creature, from the tiniest microbe to the most complex organism, is essentially the same on Earth," she continued. "Humans and animals may appear to be physically different…particularly if you compare man with an elephant or a sperm whale…but we're all structured in the same way, from the same DNA."

"I already know that, Doctor."

"The discovery of an entirely new lifeform…not found on

Earth...changes all that. We're no longer limited to studying just humans and animals; now we have a chance to look at life on another world," she persisted.

Ryan shook his head, clearly not impressed with her argument and becoming more and more annoyed with each word she spoke.

"The Jovian lifeforms are the product of millions of years of divergent evolution in a planetary environment quite different from our own," Takahashi added.

"That's exactly my point!" Westin exclaimed. "The vast differences that separate us from them...in terms of communication, technology and sociology...also reveal just how narrow-minded we are when it comes to accepting that which is not human. In fact, we may have to expand our limited definitions of what determines sentient life. Is it merely intelligence? Self-realization? Are those humans who are mentally challenged less sentient than those who are not? Perhaps there are no precise tests yet, no empirical proof that I can show you now, that will convince you otherwise. But we're dealing with something very special here."

Ryan put his hands up in the air like a traffic cop. "Doctor Shibata, do you agree with this assessment?"

"I think Doctor Westin's theory is highly speculative at best, but it does pose a number of interesting questions," Shibata replied after a long, drawn-out moment of reflection.

"Sonuvabitch!" Rachel exclaimed as she turned to walk away. Then she came back around, shoved past Ryan and went nose to nose with Shibata. "You've spent so much time up Takahashi's ass that you wouldn't know a genuine theory if you stumbled over it!"

"*Taiteki!*" Shibata glared.

"All right, that's enough." Ryan intervened, pulling them apart. "We're here to find answers, not assign guilt."

"Yeah, right," Westin said under her breath, turning around

and walking back to her science station. She plopped down in her chair and resumed her intensive study of atmospheric conditions.

Ryan ignored her and focused on the Japanese technician.

"Have you recorded any empirical data or personally witnessed any behavior that would suggest the Jovians are sentient?" he asked.

Shibata ran his hands through his long black hair and pulled the loose ends away from his face into a ponytail. Then he secured his hair with the rubber band he was wearing around his left wrist.

Finally, at last composed, he said, "The Jovian lifeforms are very elusive. They start to approach the Platform, then break off for no apparent reason. It's difficult to observe them, or record any empirical date, when they are so easily frightened away."

"You mean to say they're bashful?"

"Yes, Mister Ryan, that is precisely what I mean," he replied, looking from Ryan to Takahashi to Westin. "But in the last few months one of them, in particular, has come very close to the observation window on several occasions. If I did not know any better, I would say that 'he' is very curious..."

"Bashful? Curious?" Ryan repeated, interrupting him. "Those are human emotions, Doctor. Are you trying to tell me that these Jovian lifeforms behave like human beings?"

"I can think of no other way to describe their actions."

Ryan shook his head. "And you agree with this assessment, Doctor Takahashi?"

"Yes, I do," she replied.

"What about telemetry?" he asked, beside himself. "You must have recorded something on these creatures."

"Nothing," Shibata said.

"Maybe it's the fault of your equipment." Ryan was grasping at straws. "Are you certain your computers are working?"

"There's nothing wrong with my machines. They're all fully functional," the third technician interjected, tipping the baseball cap on his head proudly.

Bearded and prematurely balding, Leonard Provenzo fit the profile of a typical computer geek. He hadn't always wanted to be a computer technician. His shining moment had come and gone twenty-five years earlier during the counterculture revolution. A Long Island lad, he had produced an underground newspaper which professed the joys of a tri-sexual lifestyle, then got busted with two underage strippers. When the revolution ended, he moved into his parent's basement and studied computers.

"What about the remote sensors?" Ryan persisted.

"Online and active," Provenzo replied. "They should have been triggered the last time Cloud Dancer appeared."

"Cloud Dancer?"

"Mister Ryan," Takahashi explained, "Cloud Dancer is the name we have given to the Jovian lifeform that has been observed most often."

"Well, all of this is damned peculiar," Ryan concluded. "Fully functional machines that aren't functional. Sensors that should record data...and don't. I don't know what to make of any of it."

"Sensors record only that which they are programmed to record," Shibata said as a matter of fact. "The whole of the universe is infinite and there is still so much that we do not know."

"I see. So it's possible the sensors are working just fine. They're just not recording any data on these so-called Jovian lifeforms."

Shibata nodded at the former Senator.

"Does anyone have anything else to add?" Ryan asked. "Doctor Takahashi? Doctor Shibata? Doctor Westin?"

They all paused for a moment, like setting cement, and

stared off into space as if trying to recall something they may have overlooked. Then his last words finally filtered through the cerebral cortex and triggered an expression on Rachel Westin's face. She smiled broadly.

"Lenny, why don't you tell Mister Ryan what you discovered the last time you ran an equipment diagnostic?" she said, with an impish grin.

Ryan looked from Rachel to Provenzo who was hovering over one of the displays in front of him. At first, the computer technician didn't respond. He acted like he was far away in his own little world. Then, finally, he looked up and realized that they were all waiting for him.

Provenzo reported: "The voltage meter of the electrostatic shield generator recorded readings well off the scale."

"What does that mean?" Ryan asked.

"Normally, the electrically-charged particles from Jupiter's atmospheric conditions are processed through a hollow conducting sphere...about the size of a waste basket...at the base of the Platform."

"Like a weather vane?" Ryan clarified.

"Yes," the computer technician replied. "But when the electrostatic discharges exceed the shield's nominal standards, the voltage meter records those readings automatically for future study and evaluation."

"So, what you're saying is that you're getting more lightning strikes than usual."

"Yes, and with greater intensity, I might add."

"I still don't understand," Ryan confessed. "What does all that have to do with the Jovian lifeforms?"

"Well, if you compare the frequency of the..."

"The sensors may not be recording the comings and goings of our neighbors out there," Westin interrupted, cutting him off in mid-sentence, "but the meter on the shield generator certainly is."

"That's a pretty far stretch, don't you think, Doctor? Now, you're beginning to sound like Doctor Takahashi. She also thinks the Jovians are trying to communicate with electrostatic discharges. Maybe we've simply angered the god Jupiter and he's getting even with us by hurling lightning bolts at the Platform," he said, and watched the woman's glare intensify.

They looked at one another for a moment.

"Sheer fantasy, Doctor. Nothing more," he added.

Rachel Westin started to respond, then reconsidered. Instead she turned back to her monitor and resumed her data analysis…obviously annoyed.

"Well, does anyone else have something to add?"

Ryan glanced around the compartment waiting for a response, but Takahashi and Shibata were silent.

"Well, then, you've got just three days to make a believer out of me," Ryan said, turning to each of them and pointing at his watch. "Remember, that's all the time that you have left."

5

Several hours later, as the *Montgolfier* emerged from the upper stratum of clouds of the Jovian atmosphere, the Pilot announced, "We're making our final approach to the Station. Please check your safety belts."

Ryan complied and pulled the belt tight over his shoulders and across his lap. He nodded at the Pilot who did not seem as friendly or as talkative as the previous one. She remained distant as she maneuvered the craft into place by firing the retro rockets.

A few minutes later, he caught a glimpse of the Space Station, its polished metal surface shimmering with glints of yellow and red from the relatively dim star that crept over Jupiter's horizon. At nearly three hundred yards in diameter, the massive structure seemed to float in the upper cloud stratum. Its central axis—supported from below by a nuclear reactor and connected by a long, narrow cone—rotated with a slight tilt through the billowing sea of clouds that swirled up from the planet. The rising towers and spires that dotted the Space Station's upper half reached toward the stars, thousands of twinkling lights in the night sky.

When they were less than a few yards away, Ryan watched through the porthole as the docking arms extended toward the small craft. He felt a slight jolt as they took hold, then listened for the familiar sound of metal clanging against metal. Within moments, the *Montgolfier* was secure, the airlock was open, and a man wearing an orange fatigue was helping Ryan climb out. The Pilot pushed past him in a stern almost rough manner and continued walking at a fast pace out of the docking bay and into an adjacent corridor.

Ryan struggled to stand on his own two feet, then dismissed the dockworker with a nod. The former Senator closed his eyes and took in a deep breath, drinking in the rich oxygen of the Space Station. *How strange it was to be breathing real air again*, he thought.

"Haha! Haha!"

Ryan whirled around to see who was crying out "Mommy" in Japanese and spotted a little boy who had pushed through a handful of dockworkers and Security Personnel, and was racing toward the airlock, shouting *"Okasan-wa?"*—the equivalent of "Where's my Mommy?" in his native tongue. Ryan guessed the child was Doctor Takahashi's son, but wondered what had compelled the little boy to come down to the dock to search for his mother so late at night. Cramden and a handful of his elite Security Personnel followed in close pursuit, and in no time at all had the youngster surrounded on all sides.

"Sorry, sir," Cramden said, nearly out of breath. "He got by our security station and all of our usual checkpoints."

"Clever little boy," Ryan remarked, amused. "Perhaps I should put him in charge of security."

"It won't happen again, sir."

Ryan pushed through the circle of men dressed in riot helmets and black fatigues, and crouched down on one knee so he could look straight into the child's tear-filled eyes and put a consoling hand on his shoulder.

"*Dochira-sama desho ka*?" Ryan asked the boy his name, reaching back into his memory for the few Japanese phrases he had learned in college.

"Hiroshi," the little boy replied, crying.

"*Ah*, Hiroshi-*san*," he repeated gently. "*Watashi wa* Mitchell Ryan."

The boy blinked, and the blank look in his face told Ryan that he was unfamiliar with the name.

"*Do shita n desu ka?*" Ryan asked.

At his request, Hiroshi told him exactly what was wrong. Even though Ryan was only able to follow bits and pieces of the confusing jumble of nonsense words and childspeak, he learned that the child had been frightened by strange images that appeared on his bedroom wall. He tried reassuring the little boy that everything would be all right, that he was probably just dreaming, and that dreams could not hurt him. Ryan even offered to put him into contact with his mother through the Platform's comlink, but the boy just looked at him with big brown questioning eyes. The more he spoke, the more confused and upset he became.

"*Wakarimasu ka*," Ryan said, hoping he understood.

"*Hai*," Hiroshi replied, thanking him with a polite bow.

Ryan stood up, took the child's hand, and started to say, "Now, let's go find your grandmother," but before all the words could be fully spoken, the little boy broke free of his grasp and ran toward the exit. Impulsively Ryan made a lunge for him, then thought better of it when he saw the figure of a diminutive Asian in her late fifties or early sixties just beyond the exit of the docking bay. She was an attractive woman with the same porcelain features and deep, penetrating eyes as Yukiko Takahashi, and he concluded that she was Hiroki's grandmother Suki. She did not acknowledge Ryan or anyone else, nor did she say a word to the little boy or hug him; she merely took his hand and turned to walk away.

"Missus Takahashi, my name is Mitchell Ryan," he said, moving to the exit in an attempt to force an introduction. "I wanted to say what a pleasure it is to meet you, and to tell you how much you honor me with your presence."

Suki Takahashi ignored him and continued on her way. For just an instant, Hiroki turned to look back, made eye contact with Ryan, smiled, then turned and continued walking obediently with his grandmother. In a moment, they had disappeared into the darkness of the corridor.

"Well, if that doesn't beat all…" Ryan said to himself.

"Suki's always been an odd sort of person," Cramden reported as his Security Team began to disperse. "She keeps mostly to herself and doesn't socialize much with anyone outside of Doctor Takahashi and the little boy. I've never seen her at any of the Station's functions. She doesn't go to chapel. And as far as I can tell, her only function here is to watch over the boy. Quite honestly, I've had my suspicions about her loyalty for some time."

"Suspicions?"

"Antisocial types, like her, are usually the ones recruited by terrorist organizations. She could be a member of one of those environmental factions trying to shut the Station down."

Ryan shook his head incredulously.

"Want me to keep her under a twenty-four hour watch, sir?"

"No, Cramden," he replied. "Just see that she and the boy get safely back to their quarters."

"Right."

Cramden pulled two men from his Security Team and sent the rest back to their stations. He and his two men then exited the docking bay, following closely after Suki Takahashi and Hiroki. The dockworkers also began to disperse as the excitement was all over.

Ryan turned to the exit.

"What was that all about?" a voice demanded from one of the darkened recesses of the docking bay.

"Ghosts. Nightmares. Bad dreams," he groaned, feeling a sudden chill, "just like the one I'm having now." Ryan's attention was drawn into the darkness by the familiar voice. "I told you I never wanted to see your face again."

The portly figure of Edward Reinhardt emerged from the dark shadows. He was an elderly man, perhaps sixty-five or seventy, who sweated profusely. He had the skin and body of a man who had spent a lifetime living in the shadows and looked like someone who had not seen the direct rays of the sun for decades. His hair was white and his eyes were a milky pink. Ryan often thought that he could have been easily mistaken for a vampire from one of the old silent thrillers. Both had traveled in the same circles, but Reinhardt rarely moved far beyond the shadows.

Ryan starred at him with disbelief.

The portly man walked up close to him, straining his eyes to see in the darkness of the docking bay. "Now, what kind of gratitude is that for the man who made you what you are?"

"Reinhardt, I'm through paying my debt to you," he replied, "and those you represent."

Abruptly, Ryan turned his back on him and strode into the quiet corridor that connected the docking bay with the command center. His destination was the administrative offices, where he reckoned his aide was probably waiting for him with a handful of trivial concerns. He was not about to stop.

"Ryan!" Reinhardt shouted, following after him.

The former Senator ignored him and kept walking, with great purpose, down the white padded corridor toward the Central Core. At the end of the corridor, he opened the hatch which led to the Central Core and the lifts beyond.

"Ryan!" Reinhardt cried, reaching the corridor just as Ryan was half way toward the hatch. He could not walk any faster and found it difficult to keep up with Ryan's steady pace. "Ryan!" he cried out again.

Ahead of him, Ryan climbed through the hatch and disappeared into the Central Core. Reinhardt was winded and tried to catch his own breath. He was still a few seconds behind Ryan and struggled at redoubling his efforts to keep pace.

Ryan entered the hatch and walked across the Central Core. He headed for the bank of lifts on the far side and pushed the "UP" button. Now it was just a race against time: would the elevator reach his floor and allow him to escape, or would he have to turn and face his pursuer?

Reinhardt stumbled through the hatch. "Ryan," he cried. "You're not through until we say you're through!"

Dully, Ryan shook his head. He was going to have to turn and face him.

"What do you want from me?" he asked.

Reinhardt grinned, his mouth a lost graveyard, the pearly white teeth standing like forgotten tombstones in the darkness. "The mining platform," he replied. He watched momentarily as the veins on Ryan's temples pulsated with an inner rage, then added, "Some of the corporate investors are very nervous. They're worried that the Platform won't be fully operational next Monday, what with all the terrorist activity on Mars and rumors of some kind of ecological protest here. They're afraid they might actually loose money on their investment."

"You can assure them that I've got everything under control."

"That's not what I heard," Reinhardt remarked. He took a handkerchief out of his pocket and wiped his brow with it. "I heard you were having a problem with the project's scientists."

"Nothing that I can't deal with."

Reinhardt pulled him discreetly to one side. He glanced back and forth, surveying the corridor for other listeners. When he was satisfied they were alone, he looked at Ryan. "Takahashi is a liability," he said bluntly.

Incredulous, Ryan took a deliberate step backwards.

"She's just a damned idealist, that's all. She doesn't pose any real threat to the project. I can handle her and her staff."

"You don't seem to realize that she's already a threat," he insisted, under no uncertain terms. "Her preliminary report has already raised certain concerns among environmental groups back on Earth. There's even talk among certain members of the United Planets Security Council of a special commission to look into her allegations that the mining operation will threaten a new and potentially friendly lifeform. Her continued presence on the Platform just makes matters worse. Takahashi must be discredited…or silenced permanently."

"I said I could handle her."

"I'm afraid that's no longer an option."

"What are you going to do? Throw her out an airlock without a pressure suit?"

"Well, that's entirely up to you, isn't it?"

"Up to me?" Ryan demanded, reacting just like a man who had narrowly missed stepping into a bear trap. Reinhardt was twisting the meaning of his words. "What the Hell's that supposed to mean? What's up to me?"

"I don't care how you handle it. Just do it quietly."

"What are you talking about?"

Reinhardt coughed into his handkerchief. "This recycled air is not very good for my asthma. The chill always gives me a cold."

"Fuck the recycled air. I want to know what you're talking about."

"You're a smart man. You'll know what to do. "

Reinhardt's eyes narrowed, his gaze judging him with a look he knew all too well. For an instant Ryan wanted to think this was all just some kind of bad dream and that he would be waking soon. But as he examined the gaze more carefully, he realized that Reinhardt meant business.

"Don't give me that look," he said firmly. "I'm not one of your cold-blooded assassins." Ryan said as he pushed him away with both hands. "You may think that just because you bought me a few elections and got me seats on a couple of key Congressional committees that you own me. But I've long since paid that debt. I'm my own man now…and I alone decide what's in my best interests."

Reinhardt coughed again into his handkerchief. "It's getting chilly here and that's very bad for my asthma."

"I want nothing to do with your dirty deals, and I'll not stand by and watch you murder an innocent woman."

At that moment, one of the elevators from the bank of lifts chimed and its door whisked open. Reinhardt shuffled toward it, blowing his nose into his handkerchief. "You seem to act as if you had some choice in the matter," he concluded, stepping into the lift and closing the door.

Ryan pounded his fist in anger on the bulkhead. Long ago, he had promised himself that, if he ever managed to wriggle free of Reinhardt and men that he represented, he'd never again do anything questionable. He felt that he had managed to achieve that by resigning his Congressional seat and accepting the appointment to the Station. Little did he realize at the time, what was fast becoming apparent to him now. He had simply changed one venue for another where the stakes were even higher than before.

Ryan walked over to one of the Station's many comlinks

and dialed security. "Hello, this is Mitchell Ryan," he said into the microphone. He paused for a moment, trying to think of what to say, then surprised himself. "Cramden, when you get through escorting the little Asian boy and his grandmother back to their quarters, there's something I want you to do."

"Right away, sir," the voice replied.

In the corridor, just beyond the hatch to the Central Core, a figure stirred. He had been standing in the shadows, listening to the conversation between Ryan and Reinhardt with his ear to the wall. His face was completely obscured by shadows. In his right hand, he held a long, thin-bladed knife, but he simply stood there, watching and waiting and listening....

6

Yukiko Takahashi stood alone at the great circular window of the forward observation chamber, her petite Asian form dwarfed by the vast ocean of dense gas and floating clouds. She looked out the window and watched as several Jovian lifeforms broke through the clouds over an atmospheric storm system and propelled themselves carelessly across the sky. She recognized the one nicknamed Cloud Dancer by his distinctive locomotion and wanted to touch him, to know that he was real. But as she stretched her arms out against the glass to embrace him, the Jovian began moving away, out of her field of vision.

Tears were in her eyes and starting to roll down her cheeks as his silhouette faded into the distance. Her vision blurred, and she angrily swiped her forearm across her face. The smear of teardrops glistened beneath the fine, dark hairs of her arm, changing color with the red and brown hues of Jupiter.

Desperately, she pressed her hands against the cold glass, shielding her eyes to peer deeper into the clouded sea, but the lifeforms were no longer there.

She heard the sound of footsteps and turned, still crying.

Masaki Shibata stood in the entrance to the chamber. "Mister Ryan has returned to the Station," he reported in Japanese.

She stared at him with complete incomprehension.

"You wanted me to let you know…"

"Yes, yes, I remember," she replied, biting her lower lip to keep it from trembling. "Now, please leave me alone."

"Kiko-*san*, what's wrong? Why are you crying? Did I say something that upset you?" he asked, moving to her side.

Shibata tried to show that he understood what she was feeling by putting his arm around her, but she shrugged him off.

Unblinking, she stared back out the window.

"I want to know what's going on," he insisted. "Please tell me what's wrong."

Takahashi felt confused, angry, agitated, embarrassed—a hundred different emotions all at once. But her sense of dignity prevailed.

"I just want to be alone for a while," she replied, again drying her eyes with her forearm. "Thank you for your concern."

"Concern?" repeating the word like a man who had just been mortally wounded, "I thought we were closer than that, but maybe I was wrong."

"Oh, Masaki!" she cried and burst into tears once more. She turned back to him and buried herself in his embrace. "Please…no questions. I do not want to talk. Just hold me."

Shibata just held her.

Tuesday

7

Ryan opened the door to his cabin and stumbled over the two travel bags he had dropped near the entrance the day before. He was more tired than he realized and quickly changed his mind about ordering a nightcap from his personal steward. Instead, he decided to get some sleep and surveyed the rather Spartan-like quarters for something that resembled a bed. He blinked twice and stood motionless in the total darkness of his cabin. *Ah, there it is*, he sighed to himself, pulling his tie away from the collar of his shirt.

From out of the darkness, a pair of hands reached for Ryan, just as a vague, indeterminate form crept noiselessly to embrace his shadow on the far wall of his cabin. Ryan did not see the shadows on the wall, nor did he sense the presence of another person. His only thoughts were focused on reaching the bed and hitting the pillow. But as he proceeded to unbutton his shirt, the pair of hands continued to reach for him, closing in, like the noiseless, patient spider and its prey.

Just then, out of the corner of his eye, he glimpsed the shadow…and felt the tiny hairs rise on the back of his neck. Suddenly, every nerve ending in his body crackled to life, as if he had just gotten a full jolt of 110 volts of electricity from touching a faulty extension cord. The terror that burned and sizzled through his mind was real enough, but was the threat a real one or just the play of light on the wall. He turned around very slowly, so as to give the bad feeling plenty of time to go away, but he had no such luck. His sensory information registered in nanoseconds, each one progressively worse than the last, until he had turned completely around.

Ryan's eyes came down to lock on the face of his shadowy assailant and they shared a moment of mutual paralysis and recognition…then Rachel Westin embraced and kissed him deeply.

"I thought you'd never get here," she whispered, kissing him again and nuzzling his neck.

Ryan slipped out of Rachel's embrace and staggered backwards towards the door. He stood in the entrance, breathing in a deep sigh of relief. His body was still reeling from the shock of her surprise visit, but he didn't want her to know that. He had spent far too much of his political life proving how much he was in control, and he dared not show a single ounce of weakness to her or anyone else. He felt himself regaining control of the situation. *So much for things that go bump in the night*, he thought, turning to bolt the security lock on his cabin door.

"If I had known you were the welcoming committee," he said finally, "I would have come sooner."

"You always know the right thing to say," Rachel purred, walking over to him and snaking her arms around his waste. Her robe was open and she brushed her bare breasts against his shoulder blades.

"I'm a politician…remember."

"Hmmmmmmmmm…"

They turned slowly in each other's arms as they kissed. Then he reached under the oversized terry-cloth bathrobe she was wearing and gingerly pushed it away from her shoulders. The bathrobe fell to the floor at her feet and she took a step away from it, without thought or hesitation. Naked, Rachel smiled knowingly, and ran her hands from her belly to her breasts with an inviting, languorous gesture that told Ryan the stunning, five-foot-ten, Aryan blonde was his for the taking. And as she sighed and curled around him, he sighed and held her tight. Her big, beautiful breasts pressed sweetly against the buttons on his open shirt, and her long, luscious legs wrapped tightly around the pant legs of his trousers.

Ryan kissed her deeply, then moving his kisses around to her right side, he whispered in her ear, "You know, you came on pretty strong down there today."

"Like you would have noticed."

"I notice more than you give me credit for," he said.

"When have you ever seen me as more than a beautiful woman you wanted to fuck?" she asked bluntly.

Ryan tried to pull away from her embrace, but Rachel held onto him tightly, with a passionate, almost violent, sensuality that he had never found in any other woman. Her eyes burned into him, red-rimmed and horrible, and yet somehow…soft. Yes, soft and wanting. She wanted him, and he needed her…in the worst way, but for more than just a sexual partner.

"I specifically requested your transfer to the Station as its science officer," he said to her, at last.

"Well, that's a big surprise," she replied, still kissing and nuzzling him. "In the last twenty years, when have we been more than a few months apart? You've arranged for every placement I've ever had."

"Because you're competent at what you do, and because you're someone I can trust."

"I thought it was that you liked having me around to fuck."

Ryan recoiled instantly and she feigned being hurt. He was surprised by her bluntness, but not too surprised. Rachel was always blunt. That was one of the reasons why he had fallen in love with her. She brought her hands up to his face and gently stroked the coarse bristles of his five-o'clock shadow.

"Let's just be honest with each other about one thing," she whispered. "You arranged for my transfer here so that we could be together."

"Yes," he confessed, "but that's just one of the fringe benefits of having a science adviser as beautiful as you."

"Like I said, you always know the right thing to say."

Once again, Rachel took his face into her hands and kissed him deeply. Ryan groaned and fell into her arms, pressing into her breasts. While they continued kissing, she unbuttoned the rest of the buttons on his shirt, slipped the shirt over his shoulders and let it fall to the floor. Then she reached down, unfastened his belt, and unzipped the fly to his trousers. He opened his eyes to stare at her.

"Oh, Mitchell," she breathed, with a heavy sigh. "I love you...I need you..."

But Ryan broke their embrace. He put a finger to her lips, then rushed past her to the bathroom.

"Hold that thought," he exhaled. "I'll be right back."

"Don't be long, lover," she sighed as she slid gracefully over to the bed. She pulled down the black-and-white comforter that covered the bed, coyly seductive, and slipped between the sheets. As she adjusted the pillows behind her back and listened to him humming loudly from the bathroom, her eyes glimpsed a copy of the report she had filed on the Jovians sitting on his desk. The seal hadn't been broken and it was obvious to her that Ryan had never even opened it. For an instant, she dropped the thin veneer and cursed him under her breath.

"You know, Doctor Takahashi is right," she said finally.

Ryan glanced out of the bathroom.

"Did you come here to make love, or to talk about those damned Jovian lifeforms?"

Rachel waited for him to go back into the bathroom, then raised her forefinger at him. "Well, to tell you the truth," she said, "I thought we'd fuck…then while you're in the throws of passion, I'd read my science report to you."

"In your dreams…"

"You haven't changed a bit."

"Oh?"

She grumbled to herself, "You're still the same self-absorbed, tight-assed bureaucrat I met in Paris twenty years ago."

Ryan flushed the toilet and came out of the bathroom, pulling his white undershirt over his head. He stopped for a moment to check himself in the mirror, then approached the bed.

"Those were good days," he remarked.

"Good days? I'm surprised you remember them. You certainly couldn't remember my name. You kept calling me 'France.'"

"I meant it with affection."

"And I suppose you just simply called the next one Belgium," Rachel grunted, "or was it Germany?"

"You know there wasn't a next one."

She nodded, red-faced and angry. "You're right! You're the only man I've ever known who was faithful to his wife *and* his mistress."

Rachel sat up in bed, but she was still too pissed off to look him in the eyes. When he leaned down to kiss her, she turned her face up to his with her eyes already closed.

"I'm glad that you're here," he said, his lips disengaging from hers.

"So am I," she lied.

He slipped out of his boxer shorts and climbed into bed. Then he kissed her again deeply, gingerly pulling the covers back with one hand and fondling her breast with the other. Rachel smelled sweet, like fresh orchids, and as he buried his face between her thighs, he felt her hips undulating up and down. Her breasts were still full and heavy, and continued to respond to his fondling, her nipples hard as thimbles. Her belly was firm and quivering, and she responded to his wet lower kisses by clawing at the sheets with her sharp fingernails. She closed her eyes and settled deeply into the mattress as his tongue found the inner recesses of her body.

In the empty corridor, outside Ryan's cabin, a figure waited in the shadows. Isolated by the darkness, he seemed to blend right into the wall. He stood completely motionless. Only the sound of approaching footsteps caused him to stir. With a subtle move, the figure slid a long, thin-bladed knife out of his jacket and into his hand. He did not bare the knife, nor make any other kind of threatening move. He just watched and waited and listened. When he heard the footsteps pause, then finally turn away, he relaxed slightly and put the knife away. He then continued to watch and wait and listen.

8

In another part of the Space Station, near the grand Presidential Suite, Reinhardt walked alone down the corridor to his quarters. A white handkerchief was in his hand and he kept mopping his brow with it. As he approached the door to the suite, he was instantly surrounded by several, very large men in black suits. He did not react with fear or apprehension; in fact, he didn't react at all. He was not the least surprised to see them.

"She wants you," the first man said.

"Is that so?" Reinhardt replied.

"She demands an update," the second man added.

"You can tell her that I've got everything under control."

"Perhaps you'd better place that call to Earth yourself, Mister Reinhardt," the first man suggested.

Reinhardt coughed into his handkerchief. "This recycled air is bad for my asthma," he said.

"Sir?" the second man asked.

Reinhardt coughed again. "The chill always gives me a cold."

"We must not keep her waiting," the first man said.

Reinhardt looked from the first man to the second and sighed. "Do you have any idea what day and time it is in Baltimore?"

"No, sir," the first man replied.

"No, sir," the second man repeated.

"It's Monday. Yesterday. Three A.M. Eastern Standard Time," he grunted. "I'll make the call tomorrow. After Ryan's speech."

"Sir, she's not going to like that," the first man interjected.

"Now, that's not your problem, is it?"

Reinhardt forced his way through the huddle of very large men in dark suits. He unlocked the door to his suite, entered, and closed the door behind him.

9

Ryan had spent most of the morning touring the medical facility with Doctor Vasili Rudenko. Ryan had known the Russian surgeon, but not very well, back in Baltimore when Rudenko taught at Johns Hopkins University Hospital. They had both traveled in similar circles and had exchanged pleasantries, but little more, over cocktails at innumerable fundraisers, both inside and outside the Beltway. He knew bits and pieces of the Russian surgeon's background, but it wasn't until Ryan had been assigned to take over the Station that he read Rudenko's file. Apparently, Doctor Vasili Rudenko was the great-grandson of the celebrated Russian cosmonaut Tatiana Rudenko, the first woman to step foot on Mars. He had spent most of his early life working in a poorly funded hospital in St. Petersburg, spending much of his family's fortune on medical supplies and equipment. When he lost his wife and daughter in the civil war with Mars, Rudenko enlisted in the service as a Medical Officer and served with great distinction. For the last five years, he had been the Chief Medical Officer of the Space Station.

Ryan felt assured that he was the right man for the job as he and Rudenko walked towards the exit from sickbay.

"Well, thanks for the tour, Doctor," he said, smiling with a broad grin. "You've got a fine facility here and a top-notch staff. Please extend my compliments to them."

"Thank you. I certainly will," Rudenko replied, extending his hand to Ryan which he, in turn, shook.

"Perhaps we can have lunch in a few days, once all of the hoopla is over, and talk about those cocktail parties back in Baltimore."

"I look forward to that, Mister Ryan."

All at once, the long, overhead fluorescent lights began flickering madly, static charges floating up and down the tubes, plunging the medical facility in and out of darkness. Every time the lights went out, there was a collective gasp as everyone in sickbay took a deep breath, seemingly at the same time, then released it in a loud sigh as the lights came back on. Thunder, followed close at hand by lightning, rumbled through the overhead bulkhead like a summer storm. One stray spark triggered the fire detectors and within a heartbeat, it was raining water from the sprinkler system above. What made matters worse, the fire alarm screeched wildly like some forgotten banshee exposed to sunlight for the first time.

"What the Hell," Ryan said as one of the female technicians ran past him with her hands over her ears.

Rudenko stood, looking all around. "All right, people," he shouted, then crossed his arms in an authoritative stance. "We've been through this before. There's no reason to panic. Get back to your duty stations and prepare for the usual onslaught of cuts and abrasions."

Ryan nodded his approval.

"And will someone turn that damned alarm off!" he added. "How's a person supposed to think with all that goddamned noise!"

Suddenly, the two men were startled by an explosion, then loud banging noises from around the next corner.

"Come on!" Ryan exclaimed as he started running through the strobing darkness with Rudenko close behind.

They rounded the corner to find a whole bank of storage compartments moved away from the bulkhead and sitting in the middle of the corridor, vibrating up and down, banging the floor. It was as if they had all suddenly come alive and were celebrating their new found mortality with some ancient tribal dance. Three of Cramden's Security Force were pushing and pulling the vibrating metal wall, trying to wrestle it back to where it had been.

"Has the whole universe gone insane!" Rudenko exploded.

Ryan looked up and down the corridor. His Station Personnel were scurrying back and forth, attempting to contain the damage. Thankfully, no one appeared to be seriously hurt, and whatever injuries were largely superficial scrapes and cuts. Thunder was rolling down the hall, followed by the occasional burst of lightning. The overhead lights continued to blink on and off. Ryan stood there for a moment, trying to put it all together in his mind.

Just then, one of the compartments near them blew open with a bang. Without a moment's hesitation, Ryan grabbed

Rudenko by the collar and pulled him out of the line of fire of the flying debris. The two men tumbled to the deck, splashing down safely into a puddle of water.

Almost as quickly as the event began, it came to an end. The thunder subsided and the lightning stopped. The overhead lights in the corridor and throughout the Station tinkled back to life.

"Don't tell me that was some kind of electrostatic discharge," Ryan said, climbing to his feet and brushing the dust and beads of water from his Armani suit. He had a small cut on his forehead that was bleeding.

Rudenko struggled to stand. "Okay, I won't," he replied, glancing up. He took note of Ryan's wound and pulled a handkerchief from the pocket of his smock, then placed it into Ryan's hand and pressed it to his forehead.

"The simple fact of the matter is that we don't really know what it is. Come on. Let's go back to my office."

10

A few moments later, Doctor Rudenko was mixing two liquid compounds together in a large glass beaker in his office. Ryan sat on the other side of his desk, still holding the handkerchief to his head.

"What's that?" Ryan asked, beginning to feel uneasy. "I didn't say there was anything else wrong with me."

Rudenko kept right on mixing. "I understand you experienced some dizziness and disorientation on your first trip down to the Platform yesterday."

"That's right," Ryan replied, defensively. "But from what Cramden tells me, everyone does. He says the dizziness and nausea have something to do with a person's respiratory system reacting to the gases. I'm sure I'll be fine the next time I take the trip down there."

"Oh, I concur with his diagnosis. Definitely," he said, now pouring the mixture into a small glass. "I'm sure you'll be just fine."

"Well, I'm glad you do, Doctor. I had a complete physical workup just before I left Earth eighteen months ago, and the medical team there felt that I was in excellent shape for a man of fifty," Ryan stated. "I don't like doctors. I never have. And I prefer not to be poked or prodded by you or anyone else at this point..."

Rudenko dropped two solid, clear cubes in the glass and swilled them around in the liquid before handing the glass to Ryan.

"What the Hell is that?" he asked, holding the glass up to the fluorescent lights. "Ice?"

Rudenko grinned. "Who wants a warm vermilion cloud-burst?"

"What makes you think I need a drink?"

"Well, I've always thought that sometimes a patient feels more comfortable talking to his bartender than his doctor," Rudenko replied, pouring a drink for himself. Then he clanked his glass against Ryan's and added, "Cheers."

"Cheers!" the former Senator repeated and drank a deep gulp.

For a moment, both men sat in silence, then Rudenko asked, "Why don't you talk to me as your bartender and tell me what's really on your mind?"

"I'm not sure," he confessed.

Ryan glanced at Rudenko, but wouldn't meet his eyes. He wanted to ask the Chief Medical Officer something, but didn't quite know how to go about it. Finally, he said, "Is there anything that you can tell me about my predecessor's death?"

"Cardiac arrest," he replied. "His mechanical heart just simply stopped working one day."

"Don't you find that to be a little odd?"

"Not especially. People on Earth die of heart failure every day. Besides, Doctor Deckers, the Station's Coroner, conducted a routine autopsy of the body, and could find nothing out of the ordinary."

"Yes, I know. I read his report," Ryan said, as a matter of fact. "I also read the report you filed three months earlier on his physical condition. With the exception of his mechanical heart, Miles Bennett was perfectly healthy, in tip-top shape. In fact, he was experiencing better health than at any other point in his life. His only real complaint was a problem with sleeplessness."

"That's right," Rudenko admitted. "Bennett had insomnia. He couldn't adjust to the sleep cycles in space, like the other twenty-four percent of the personnel on this Station, and for that, I prescribed a mild sedative. But I can assure you the sedative was not responsible for his heart failure."

"Suppose he made a mistake…and forgot how many pills he had taken."

"An overdose? Not likely. Besides, had Bennett taken too many pills, it would have shown up in the toxicology screen that Deckers ran during the autopsy, but there was no report of an overdose."

Ryan sighed, and shook his head. "Every time I think I've got things figured out, something else happens that makes me question my very thought processes. I'm a rational man and expect rational explanations. I don't like mysteries. I don't like inconsistencies. And I don't like unexplained things. But right now, all I've got are a lot of questions that don't seem to have any rational answers."

"Don't you think you're being a little hard on yourself?"

"Not at all, Doctor. There are a hundred and fifty-three people stationed here and a world of eight billion back home that are counting on me to make the right decisions for them. I can't afford to make a mistake."

"Mister Ryan, mistakes are what make us human. They are what help us to grow and change and become hopefully better people," Rudenko observed. "Start treating yourself like you treat everyone else aboard this Station. Like a human being."

"Now, you sound like a doctor, bartender."

"Well, it's no wonder. We both see the same two kinds of people: those who are sick and those who are dying."

"And which one am I?"

"Well, that all depends on you, doesn't it?" Rudenko continued without waiting for a reply. "Maybe it's time you stop trying to do everyone else's job and focus on what you do best. Your people know what they have to do. They just need someone to lead them."

Ryan hung his head. "Thanks, I guess I needed to hear that. It's just that no one on my staff except you was bold enough to say it."

"One of the prerogatives of a good bartender, or a chief medical officer, for that matter, is being able to dispense wisdom, even when it's an unpopular vintage," he said, holding the beaker of martini over Ryan's glass. "Now why don't you let me pour you another drink?"

"Whatever you say, Doc."

11

Lenny Provenzo spent much of his downtime living in the shadows, stalking Rachel Westin.

Always careful to stay about twenty paces behind, he watched her through his thick glasses and made imaginary plans for their life together. On this particular day, he had followed her into the mess hall where she stopped to get a cup of coffee with friends. He tucked himself behind the counter where people stacked cafeteria trays and disposed of their trash, and stared at her with his big, brown, puppy-dog eyes. How she could carry on an intelligent, meaningful conversation with those muscle-bound lunkheads from Cramden's security force was a matter that was beyond him, but it didn't trouble his near-genius IQ for very long. He figured that once they were together as a couple she would never have to deal with the likes of them again.

In the four weeks that they had worked together on the Mining Platform and in the research labs on board the Station, Lenny had decided that Rachel Westin was the perfect woman for him. She was always sweet and had a pleasant word for him every morning, which is more than he could say for the other Station personnel who regarded him as a four-eyed geek. Whenever she came near him, his hormones went berserk, sending all sorts of uncontrollable feelings through his usually well-controlled mind. He could not help but notice her long and sleek legs, the perfect proportions of her breasts, the hourglass shape of of her body, the way that she threw her blonde hair back when no one was looking…

He had spent every waking moment noticing everything about her. He liked the fact that she was so intelligent because he knew that he could reach her on a mental level. He also liked that she was beautiful, so he would not have to feel embarrassed to be out with her; not like the trolls he often seemed to attract. And he also liked that she was popular, but not so popular that she was always surrounded by men.

Today was the day, Lenny decided, to make his move.

He adjusted the baseball cap on his head, and smoothed out the wrinkles in his baggy trousers so that he would not look too odd when he approached her for a date. Lenny's biggest disappointment in life was that he had gone prematurely bald in his early twenties and had doubted his virility ever since.

The Biblical story of Samson was all too real to him. Other men with full heads of hair always seemed to get the girls he wanted, and that left only those women that he considered to be trolls. To compensate for the lack of hair on his head, he grew a great bushy beard, but given a choice between his brains and a full hear of hair, Lenny would have taken the hair on any day of the week.

Lenny Provenzo watched and waited for his opening.

With the mess hall choked to capacity, the noise level, a low, thunder-like rumble that hung over their heads, seemed ready to pop like a sonic boom. Station personnel, in their blue and white, short-sleeved uniforms, mingled with the few residents, exchanging stories and off-color jokes. Rachel seemed to be laughing the loudest; surrounded by several tall, handsome men who were each vying for her attention, she basked in their spotlight like a nightclub performer at a gentlemen's club.

"Hey, Lenny, how are you doing?" one of the female cafeteria workers asked, as she picked up a handful of trays. She was short and plump, but had a smile that wrapped all the way across her face.

Lenny looked around nervously. "Oh, hi, Rebecca," he replied at last, praying that Rachel had not seen him with her. He regarded the short, plump cafeteria worker as one of the trolls that inevitably found him. "I can't talk with you right now. I've got something that I've gotta do."

All at once, he saw Rachel stand up and start moving past him with several other guys in tow. "Rachel!" he called.

Rachel looked back, a tiny smile on her face. A couple of her friends were laughing at a joke of hers. She waved, but kept moving.

"Rachel!" he called again and started to move after her, but Rebecca grabbed him by the arm and held him back.

"Why don't we meet sometime for a drink or something?" she asked, smiling, looking up into his eyes.

"Yeah, sure, anything," he replied, scrambling to get free of her grasp. "Look, I really do gotta go."

Apprehensive, Lenny pushed through the crowds and scurried to keep up with Rachel and her friends. They were approaching the bank of elevators at the Central Core and he'd lose her once she got inside. Now that he had his courage up, he didn't want to wait for another time. He was just preparing to climb out onto that proverbial big limb when she stopped walking and turned casually around to one of the guys in her party. Rachel spotted him and pushed her friend aside.

"Are you stalking me, Lenny?" she asked, smiling.

Provenzo froze in his tracks, his shoulders bunched up like a cartoon character that had hit an imaginary obstacle in the road.

"I've got to talk to you," he said, meekly. "Alone."

"Lenny, this may not be the right time," she replied, pointing to her friends. Each of the men regarded the bespectacled computer nerd, with his baggy pants, baseball cap and tennis shoes, as a kind of walking joke, and they had to cover their mouths to keep from laughing at him.

"We have to talk *now*," he said, with a trifle more force, cringing from the looks he saw in each of their faces.

Rachel looked annoyed. She looked past Lenny to the other friends. "I'll catch up to you guys in a couple of minutes," she said.

After the men had walked away with their laughs and snickers, she turned to stare at him, her exquisite crystalline eyes suddenly turning hard. "Okay, I hope this is worth embarrassing me in front of my friends."

"Hey, I'm sorry," he said, suddenly gone soft inside. She always had that effect on him. She was so…perfect, her long blonde hair, perfect body. "Maybe I should just talk to you later."

Rachel rolled her eyes and sighed loudly, folding her arms across her chest. "If you've got something to say, Lenny, say it.

Don't beat around the bush. I don't have all night." She wanted to add, "You'll get a sunburn basking in my radiance too long," but bit her tongue instead.

He fumbled for the right words, then asked, "How are you adjusting to things here? I mean, you know, your job and all."

"Fine," she said. "The hours are a bit longer than what I'm used to, but generally speaking, I like my new assignment."

"That's good," he remarked, unable to find the next words to say.

Rachel put her hands on her hips and raised an eyebrow. "Look, you didn't hunt me down to ask me about my job, did you, Lenny?"

He felt his stomach muscles tighten and blurted out, "I think I may have found a way to track the Jovians."

The words just shot out of his mouth before he had a chance to stop them. He sighed deeply and dropped his head in defeat. That wasn't the speech he had planned to give her, but the computer technician had completely lost his nerve to say anything else.

"What did you just say?" she asked him, then waved to one of her friends passing by.

"I think I've found a way to track the Jovians," he repeated, with hesitation. He took off his glasses and held them up, checking for smudges. "After our meeting with Mister Ryan yesterday, I started thinking about how we might use the Platform's shield generator to track their movements. By re-aligning several of the key elements in the voltage meter, we should be able to turn it into a kind of motion detector that…"

"…alerts us whenever the Jovians approach the Platform," Rachel interrupted, completing his thought.

"Exactly," he said. Now he had recovered from his feelings of defeat and was starting to get enthusiastic about her again. "By overlaying all of the data that we've gathered, such as the lightning strikes and the other, assorted anomalies, we should be able to generate a three-dimensional profile of their comings and goings. Perhaps enough to make some sense of what they want…"

"…and why they're so curious about us," she concluded. She thought about this for another moment, then said, "Maybe we're looking at this in the wrong way. Maybe we should be asking ourselves why the voltage meter goes haywire every time the Jovians approach the Platform. Why the electrostatic discharges? What purpose does the use serve them?"

"Offensive? Defensive?" Lenny hurled out a couple of ideas without thinking. He then paused to consider her questions. "Back on Earth, dolphins and whales use a sort of sonar to guide them in the ocean. Perhaps the Jovian lifeforms rely on the electrostatic discharges as a kind of navigation tool."

Rachel's eyes widened. "They may also be trying to communicate with us," she said, with a look of wonder. "Think about it. Electronic impulses from our brain control all of our autonomic functions. Maybe the Jovians have found a way to communicate with each other through electrostatic discharges."

"You know, you have just given me an idea," he added triumphantly. "What if the Jovians regard the Mining Platform as some kind of entity?"

"Yes, of course," she exclaimed, "and they've been trying to communicate with us in the only way that they know how." She glanced down at her chronometer and said, in a panic, "I'm late." She patted him on the back, then hurried on without a backward glance.

"Rachel, wait," he said, nearly running into her. "We need to test our theory."

She stopped walking and turned to stare at him. "Tomorrow," she said, then added, "Look, Lenny, I'm sorry, but I'm really late now. I promised that I would meet someone."

He looked at her with his puppy-dog eyes. "I thought that we might spend some time together…working on this."

"Tomorrow," she promised.

"But you don't understand, Rachel," he said, fumbling for the right words. "I don't want you rushing off to some late night rendezvous with another guy. I want you to spend the time with me."

Rachel swallowed hard, remembering that Lenny had been the first one to befriend her when she arrived at the Station. She remembered that she had no sooner disembarked from the shuttle than he was there offering to carry her bags and escort her to her quarters. He connected her to the main server and also made sure that she knew how to find the mess hall. And when she had come stumbling out the airship, on her first journey down to the Platform, sicker than a dog, she remembered that Lenny had taken to a restroom and held her head, while she vomited up the contents of her stomach. Lenny Provenzo had been a real friend, and she found it impossible to see him as anything other than a friend.

She looked at him, feeling bad. "Lenny," she said slowly, "I'm really flattered that you feel that way about me. Any woman in her right mind, would be lucky to have such a decent man as you in her life."

"Yeah, right," he groaned.

"I already have a boyfriend," she continued, breaking the news as gently as she could to him, "but you and I have something more special than that. You and I are friends."

"Swell," he replied. He adjusted his glasses, which had slipped down to the end of his nose, by pushing up on the center bar. "I haven't even been out on a date with you and you're already reading me the 'let's be friends' speech."

Rachel smiled. "Okay, then," she said, with a twinkle in her eyes, "why don't you be my date for the inauguration ceremony tomorrow?"

"No kidding?"

"No kidding," she reassured.

Without any hesitation, he leaned over and kissed her on the cheek. "I'll see you tomorrow!" he shouted as he scurried down the hall, his feet barely touching the carpeted floor as he ran.

Rachel's smile broadened as she continued in the opposite direction.

12

Later that night, Ryan was seated at his computer console, dictating the last few changes of his speech, when the door to his quarters chimed. He reacted to the sound with a start, then looked over at the clock on his nightstand by the bed. It was nearly midnight and he was not expecting any visitors. Of course, when he opened his door and found Rachel standing in the entrance, he should not have been too surprised, but still managed a look of wonder. She was dressed to kill in a black, low-cut evening gown, and had a bottle of wine and a cork-screw in each hand.

"Rachel," he said, after a long, silent pause.

"I don't like being stood up," she replied, coolly.

"Were we supposed to meet? I don't remember…"

"I don't like being second choice either."

Ryan saw the naughty glint in her eyes. Instantly, he knew that she was not really angry or upset with him, and smiled. She had simply been toying with him, so he continued to play along.

"No…never," he added.

"Well, then, as long as we understand each other…"

Smiling, she handed him the bottle of wine and corkscrew, then moved gingerly across the room to his bed. She kicked off her high-heel shoes. Then, in one, singular, graceful movement, she slid onto the bedspread and beckoned him to lie down beside her.

"...come here."

"Whatever you say, darling."

Ryan picked up two glasses from the top of his dresser and approached the bed, extending one of them to her. She took it, and smiled. The cork popped out of the bottle and tossed aside the corkscrew.

"There's nothing quite like getting what you want," she purred, "except perhaps getting more of what you want."

"I couldn't agree with you more."

Ryan poured them both a glass of wine, put the bottle on his nightstand, and sat down beside her . . .

In the dark recesses of the corridor, outside Ryan's quarters, a shadow moved, with no apparent corporeal form attached to it...

13

Rachel knew that morning would eventually come, and with it, she would have to go back to being the Station's Chief Science Officer, which she wasn't ready for, at least not yet. She loved the feel of the sheets against her naked skin. She rolled over to snuggle against the man who had brought her so much pleasure for those few hours during the night, only to find that his side of the bed was empty.

Ryan was across the room, sitting at his computer, working on his speech. She slipped out of bed and moved right up behind him, then placed her arms gently over his shoulders and kissed him on the cheek.

"It's really late, dear. Why don't you go back to bed?" he said simply.

"I want you to come back to bed with me," she replied, pushing open his terry-cloth robe and ranking through the hairs on his chest with her long fingernails. "I could make it very interesting for you."

He pretended to consider her words, then shook his head. "I've got too much work to do on my speech."

"You don't know what you're missing," she said playfully, moving the fingers of her hands down to his crotch.

Startled, Ryan reacted to her sexual advances by shrugging her off. "Rachel," he shouted, "that's enough."

"Oh, Mitchell, why am I so attracted to men like you?" she asked, remembering how interested and attentive Lenny had been earlier that day. "You have a kind and gentle side that surfaces every now and then, but the rest of the time, you're so driven, ruthless, and…unapproachable. I don't know why I always fall for a man like you when there are really nice guys like Lenny out there who would do anything just to have a beautiful woman love them."

"Oh, really. Should I be worried about a rival for your affection?"

"No," she replied, shocked that Ryan had even been listening. "He's just a very sweet man who told me he had a crush on me, nothing more."

"And how did he break this news to you?" he asked, glancing up from his computer. "With flowers and candy?"

"No," she said, annoyed. She paused for a moment, then added, "I ran into him in the corridor outside the mess hall. He was anxious to talk to me about a discovery that he had made about the Jovians."

"Well, that's a very novel approach," he said, bemused.

She ignored his quip and continued, "He's convinced the Jovians are using the electrostatic discharges as a way to navigate through their environment, and he has some pretty convincing evidence to support his theory."

"What do you think?" he asked, again looking up briefly from his speech.

"I agree with him; in fact, I'd go further and say that the Jovians are attempting to communicate with us in the only way that they know."

"Interesting," he said, as a matter of fact.

Rachel watched him continue to work on his computer, completely unfazed by what she had just told him. Only a few hours before, both she and Lenny had been encouraged by the potential of their theory. "Lenny's going to be my date today at the inauguration," she added, trying to see if she could get any kind of reaction out of him, "not that you would have noticed."

"I'll alert the media," he replied sarcastically.

"You're a real asshole, you know that?" she said, getting up from the bed, angry and red-faced. "I need to take a shower. I suddenly feel dirty all over."

Ryan looked up from his computer and watched her walk away.

As much as he hated to admit it, Mitchell Ryan needed Rachel Westin much more than she needed him. Over the years, he had known plenty of other women, including the usual assortment of call girls, chippies, escorts, interns and rich, devoted constituents, but Rachel was the first woman he'd really gotten close to since he had married his wife and settled down to have a family. He didn't take their extramarital affair lightly. His wife Susan and Rachel were two very different women, and the more he had grown tired of his wife, the more he realized how much he needed his mistress. Often, Susan had told him that he was a dull and uninteresting man and he had taken her words to heart, figuring there just wasn't much point in arguing with a woman who commanded such influence and power in his political circles. But when Rachel had told him differently, he realized how much he really needed her. She didn't think he was dull, laughed at all his jokes, and told him that he was a great lover in bed. Actually, he came to rely on them both: Susan for her political savvy and connections and Rachel for her unconditional love.

A faint smile came over his face as he recalled those care-free days with her in Paris some twenty years ago. He had just won his first election to Congress, narrowly beating out the incumbent in the Fourth District, and was taking a much needed two-week vacation in Europe when Rachel had come stumbling into his life, on one foot, with the heel broken on her right shoe. She had nearly fallen into his lap with the broken heel in one hand and the shoe in the other as he tried to climb out of his limousine. He was never able to fix her shoe, but on the ride back to her hotel, they had picked up on each other's loneliness and determined to solve the problem together. Like newlyweds on their honeymoon, they danced on an evening boat cruise on the Seine, kissed for the first time in the bell tower of Notre Dame Cathedral, hand-fed each other food at *Le Jules Verne* in the Eiffel Tower, and ran barefoot like two children along the Champs-Elysees during a summer cloudburst. During those few, stolen moments with her, Ryan had never felt more alive in his entire life. He knew that he couldn't leave "France" behind and made arrangements so that they would always be together.

Rachel came back into the room, her hair still wet from the shower and her face still flushed from the confrontation that she had just had with him. She looked down at him and said, "You know, I love you, Mitchell, but sometimes you just really piss me off."

Ryan smiled at her, pulling her head down on his shoulders. Then he gathered her into his arms and squeezed her naked body tight against his. He loved her, too, but somehow, the words never wanted to come out of him. In the twenty years that they had been together, he had often spoke of love, but had never once told her "I love you." It had been his problem with Susan, too. Mitchell Ryan always kept certain things bottled up inside. Rachel seemed to understand that and never pressed him.

"I couldn't imagine not having you around," Ryan finally said. "You're such an important part of my life."

She wrapped her arms around him and held him close.

Ryan kissed her, then kneaded her shoulder blades and the small of her back. He kissed her neck slowly, lingering over every inch. Rachel closed her eyes and moaned softly as they clung to each other in the darkness.

Wednesday

14

At noon on Wednesday, a crowd of two hundred people was waiting for Mitchell Ryan in the recreation hall, and everyone rose politely, clapping, as he entered behind his administrative aide. Flashbulbs exploded in his face and reporters from several networks struggled in vain to have a brief word with him. But as he strolled by, Ryan simply smiled and nodded at several familiar faces. Among those familiar faces were delegates from the United Planets, his personal staff, Yukiko Takahashi, Rachel Westin and her date Lenny Provenzo, Lloyd Cramden, and Doctor Rudenko. In the very back of the room, Edward Reinhardt stood in the shadows, together with several very large men in black suits. Noticeably absent from the gathering was Masaki Shibata.

As he smiled and waved to the crowd, Ryan whispered to his aide: "Charlie, I thought I told you I wanted to keep this small."

Charles Bradford, a young African-American in his thirties, shrugged. "Once the media was involved, I didn't have much choice."

The former Senator waved one final time at the crowd, then sat down in the front row, while his aide climbed several steps to a makeshift podium. The clapping and exaltation continued unabated for another moment or two, then Bradford raised his hands in the air and stepped up to the microphone. The crowd of well-wishers gradually quieted down, and everyone returned to their seats in an orderly fashion. The recreation hall fell silent, except for the occasional cough or whisper.

"Ladies and gentlemen," Bradford spoke into the microphone, "it gives me great pleasure to introduce the three-time Congressman and twice-elected Senator from the great state of Maryland...Mitchell Ryan."

As Ryan ascended the rostrum amidst another round of applause, he seized the opportunity to shake several hands of those nearest the stage. He waved again at the crowd and took his place at the podium. They continued to applaud him as he paused before the microphone.

"Distinguished guests, ladies and gentlemen, members of the press," he began his speech, "I want to thank you for the warm show of support you've given me during this very difficult and trying transition. My predecessor Miles Bennett was a tireless and dedicated public servant and a very capable administrator. His untimely death has left a tremendous void in the project which was first and foremost in his mind and the colony in which he was such an active and vital leader. He will most assuredly be missed. Therefore, when I was asked by the President of the United States to assume his position as the Station's Chief Administrator, I agreed to do so with some reluctance and a deep sense of duty. Although I can never begin to fill his shoes, I want you to know that I will do everything within my power to see that his dreams for this Station all come to pass."

The recreation hall resounded with applause and Ryan used the moment to whisper a sincere thanks to his aide for setting the whole thing up.

"Some years ago, when I decided to enter politics, I did so with an unflinching idealism to make my country a better place. To not only have the voice of my constituency heard on the floor of Congress but also to pass legislation that would make a difference in the lives of the average American. I tried to do just that and, over the years, the people of Maryland gave me their vote of confidence by returning me to the House several times and electing me to the Senate twice," he stated simply but elegantly. "Now I have been asked to undertake a new and challenging role with that same unflinching idealism. Though I would have preferred to have continued serving the people of Maryland in the United States Congress, I realized that I had an even greater obligation to serve all of mankind..."

While the former Senator dazzled his audience with his familiar political rhetoric, Masaki Shibata laid prostrate against the great circular window of the forward observation chamber several hundred kilometers below the Station. His arms and legs were stretched out and his face was pressed to the Plexiglas. He could barely breathe as his lungs heaved in and out. As he gasped for air, Shibata realized the mixture of oxygen and nitrogen had been somehow reverse. Instead of the two percent oxygen and ninety-eight percent other gases, he was breathing pure oxygen. The oxygen-rich air might not have proved fatal in any other environment, but under the tremendous pressure needed to maintain life support on the mining platform, the gas was far more lethal than cyanide.

Once he had started breathing it, the highly corrosive gas began burning away the inner lining of his lungs. In a matter of minutes, Shibata was literally drowning in his own lung tissue...and there was nothing he could do . . .

The sound of applause echoed in the distance.

"With the big task ahead, each one of us has an obligation to reach beyond our limitations to be more than what we are," Ryan continued. "John Fitzgerald Kennedy once said that we should put a higher premium on individual achievement and the quest for the new frontier rather than just accepting the way things are. That new solutions to old problems were more important than simply doing the right thing all the time." He glanced down at his notes, cleared his throat, and looked up again. "We've been given an important task by the people of the Earth, and they're counting on us to see that task through. We have a responsibility to try everything within our power to solve their resource problems, and keep trying until those problems no longer exist. And with your help, we will succeed."

Ryan paused one final time to drink in the adulation and applause, then launched into the final words of his speech with renewed vitality.

"I would just like to thank all of you for coming," he concluded, "and to wish you God's blessings for the months ahead."

The Recreation Hall exploded with raucous applauds and cheers as Ryan bowed, smiled and waved at the crowd from his vantage point on the stage. He was the consummate politician and, for the first time in eighteen months, he felt clearly in his own element.

As he made his way from the podium, Ryan exchanged the usual small talk and pleasantries that courtesy demanded in situations like this. He shook hands, smiled, nodded and repeated "Hello, nice of you to come" in a well-rehearsed, cordial manner. Had there been a baby in the audience, he would no doubt have kissed it. He was campaigning, not for political office, but good will.

With her hand outstretched, Rachel approached him. She seemed anxious to congratulate him, but he just brushed by her, taking the hand of the person standing next to her. For an instant, she was miffed; but when the indelible image of Monica

Lewinski hugging President Clinton flashed through her head, she thought better of her decision to connect with him.

Ryan kept moving through the crowd, glad-handing well-wishers and sidestepping questions from reporters.

"Ladies and gentlemen of the press," Bradford interceded, pushing the new Chief Administrator toward an exit from the Recreation Hall. "Mister Ryan will not be taking any questions at this time. But I will be happy to respond to any questions or comments you have."

Ryan felt obliged to take his aide's escape route and slipped out the side exit door in all of the confusion. Once in the dark service corridor, he found himself cornered by his old adversary, Edward Reinhardt.

"Congratulations," he offered, extending his right hand, "that was a most inspiring speech."

"What are you doing here?" Ryan demanded.

"Your administrative assistant has decided to take a few questions from the press, so I thought this would be a good time for us to talk."

"I don't have anything to say to you, and there's nothing you've got to say that I want to hear."

Reinhardt looked astonished. "Mitchell," he said in protest, "I just wanted to compliment you on your speech."

"Stop dancing around and just say what you've got to say."

Reinhardt leaned toward him and whispered, "I've taken care of your problem."

"Who the Hell do you think you are? God?" Ryan scowled, dropping the outward façade of civility for whoever might still be lingering about. "You just snap your fingers and problems disappear."

"Well, I only meant…"

"I know what you meant. I've been involved in politics my entire life, and I've worked too long and too hard to let someone with a misguided sense of citizenship fuck me up."

Reinhardt backed off, startled. The seventy-year-old man took a handkerchief from his pocket and mopped the perspiration from his brow. His movements were without any kind of thought or volition. They were almost instinctive, like an animal in the wild.

"Strange," he said, at last. "You didn't feel my contributions to your political career were misguided."

"Your contributions didn't have anything to do with the success or failure of my political career," Ryan replied.

"They had everything to do with it."

"I considered them gifts."

"Well, you better start realizing they were investments," Reinhardt said with some authority, "that should now yield a high return to your benefactors."

Ryan looked trapped as he desperately searched the darkened corridor for some avenue of escape. His eyes caught a fleeting glimpse of a shadow that moved near the service exit, but he could make out no discernible figure. It was there one moment, then gone the next. For an instant, he thought he was seeing things, then Reinhardt's rantings brought him back to reality.

"You owe me, Mitch," the older man concluded, "and now, I've come to collect on that debt."

"After all these years, you still haven't learned a damn thing about politics."

"I understand money."

"They're not the same."

"Since when?"

"I'm not for sale, Edward. I never was."

"A man with integrity," Reinhardt mocked him. "But please tell me where was that integrity when you first came to me with that little problem of yours." He paused for a moment of reflection. "Now, let me see if I can remember...you wanted a committee appointment..."

"Right now, my only problem is you."

"Mitch, how could you possibly say that to me? After all we've meant to each other."

"Get out of my life," Ryan shouted, "and stay out of my business."

"Oh, look at the time," he said, pretending to look at his chronometer. "We'll just have to complete this conversation at some other time. I've got to get back to my suite and change for the reception." He wiped his forehead again. "And you mustn't be late for your…coronation."

Reinhardt nodded at him and exited through the service door, leaving Ryan all alone in the darkness.

15

The reception was already in full swing when Ryan finally arrived and walked into the mess hall, wearing a black Brioni tuxedo and looking his best. He would have hardly recognized the hall, with all of the decorative banners, streamers and balloons, had it not been for the fact that he had already eaten several meals there. Amid a murmur of conversation, delegates from Earth and the Station personnel mingled, or sampled the exotic drinks, *hors d'oeuvres*, or catered food. A fantastic array of every kind of fish, fowl, meat, or vegetarian dish from many difficult cultures filled the main dining table to overflowing.

Over it all was a faint aura of edgy politeness verging on hostility. Members of the United Planets, which constituted the union of all countries on Earth and the aligned colonies of the Solar System, were concerned that the Mining Platform would open and begin excavating the precious minerals necessary for the survival of all nations on time and without incident. The likelihood of an act of sabotage by environmentalist groups and the ongoing terrorist threat from Mars were two major concerns that weighed heavily on the delegates. Rumors that one or more of the member nations had supplied weapons and the raw materials to make a dirty bomb had re-ignited old rivalries and suspicions among the delegates. Keeping open warfare from breaking out among them before the Platform even became operational was going to be a tough problem; many of them were not even trained diplomats, but merely minor officials who had been pressed into service by bosses who had refused to make the eighteen-month journey and place themselves in harm's way.

Ryan spotted Cramden and Rudenko in a group that included a Pakistani named Desai Apurva, two Spaniards called Pablo and Anca Giro, and a Lord from the British Parliament named Ian Davis. Well, at the very least, despite their vast political and social differences, they were behaving politely.

As Ryan joined the group, Cramden was saying, "Lord Davis, I understood that you had retired from public service before this event was scheduled and settled into an estate in Sutton Coldfield. Forgive my curiosity, but, as an expatriate of the United Kingdom, I'm interested in hearing your reasons for leaving such a garden paradise behind to make the grueling three-year round trip journey here."

Characteristic of people from Pakistan, Apurva was listening for his reply with his head down and slightly tilted, while the Giros, sipping snifters of brandy, were staring directly into the Lord's face. For an American unaccustomed to diplomats from either country, it would have been hard to say which of them, if either, was being rude, but Ryan had attended enough of these social gatherings to know they were simply acting like themselves. So he stood back and listened.

"The Prime Minister asked me personally to undertake this mission," he said, with a certain amount of pride and arrogance.

"The British Empire may not wield the same kind of power that it once did two hundred years ago, but that admission does not mean that we have become insensitive to the plight of savages in their own native environs. For instance, when our mighty British frigates first sailed into the waters of the Galapagos Islands, we exercised tremendous restraint rather than plunder its natural resources for our own gain. Our warships protected the area so that naturalists like Charles Darwin could explore its unspoiled beauty and make the kind of discoveries that we take so much for granted today."

"So then, you view the Jovians as some sort of noble savage that needs to be protected from our industrial progress," Cramden said.

Ian Davis shook his head. "I do not know enough about them to make that kind of judgment. That is something better left to scientists than politicians. But I would ask you to consider where we would be today if it had not been for individuals like Darwin and his discoveries in the Galapagos Islands."

Pablo Giro put his snifter down and leaned still farther forward. When he spoke, his voice was rough, grating and clumsy; English was not a language that he learned easily, yet he spoke it better than his wife Anca. "Lord Davi*es*, you opposite…I mean to say *oppose* this operation?"

"I reserve my opinion, Mr. *Jy*-ro," Davis replied, turning toward him, "but the instructions of my government are quite clear. The United Kingdom supports the mining project and the U.P. resolution that authorizes the United States to proceed with the operation despite the potential risks to the indigenous population. But I cannot help but think that we are making a mistake in not heeding the lessons of the past."

"Then you *do* oppose this operation?"

Apurva lifted his head. "Pablo, why must you push him on this matter? He has given you his answer. Let it alone." His English was letter perfect, revealing the fact that he had studied at Oxford University for several years before returning to Pakistan to enter the diplomatic service.

"No. His words…still forceful in Parliament…sways others," Giro said, stabbing a finger towards Davis. "There is…growing opposition. Talk of a new vote. Discussion of a new resolution. I will know where he stands and why."

"Spaniards are all the same. They do not argue for reasons," Davis stated. "They just simply argue."

"That is an insult…"

"Gentlemen," Ryan interrupted, stepping between them. "Lord Davis has taken precious time away from his retirement to stand with us today in unity as a representative of the United Kingdom. Just as each of you has forfeited time with your family and friends back on Earth to be here. We should honor the sacrifice that you each have made by celebrating the strengths that we all have in common and by overlooking our individual differences."

For a moment, the diplomats stared at each other, arms folded across their chests in a defensive posture. Then Davis nodded at the former Senator. "You are absolutely right, Mister Ryan. While each of us may disagree in principal with the other, we do stand united against a common foe."

"Agreed," Apurva whispered.

Pablo Giro remained rigid for a moment, then nodded and said in a gruff tone of voice, "You will excuse me," and left the group, taking his wife Anca in tow while she was still snifting brandy.

"You have met Giro before, Lord Davis," Apurva said, softly enough not to be overhead by anyone outside of the group.

"We debated at my last Council session," he replied. "The Spaniard did not agree with the resolution to blockade the Mars colony because it meant that Spain, Portugal, and Holland could no longer profit from the sale of weapons and technology to the rebel factions there."

"Ambassador Giro lost," Ryan added with a straight face. If Desai Apura was amused by the punch line, his face chose not to show it. Instead he nodded solemnly, and moved off with soft but deliberate steps.

Ian Davis looked at the former Senator. "I do want to thank you for intervening, Mister Ryan, but it was completely unnecessary."

"Lord Davis, you and I have known each other for a great many years, so you must forgive me for being blunt," he said coolly. "Your personal feelings about the Jovians are entirely inconsequential and must be kept out of his arena, for they threaten an already shaky alliance."

Davis' eyes went wide. "Really! Well, we'll just see about that, won't we?"

Several other Station personnel, besides Cramden and Rudenko, had overhead their conversation and were whispering to each other. Quickly, Lord Davis put down his glass of cognac and turned to leave.

"Excuse me, gentleman," he said to Cramden and Rudenko. "It has been a long day for me and I am suddenly feeling very fatigued." He propelled himself toward the exit amid a barrage of "good nights."

Rudenko turned back to Ryan, who did not appear to be the least bit discomforted. "Well, that could have gone a lot better."

"Doctor, do you disagree with what I said to him?"

"No," he replied, shaking his head. "I just think that you could have been a bit more tactful in how you said it."

Ryan glanced at him sharply, as though surprised, but recovered in a manner of heartbeats. "I've been dealing with diplomats and politicians like him my entire life. Some respond to discreet words and phrases, while others are only moved by a direct, forceful approach."

"Whatever you say, sir."

Just then, Rachel approached holding a Cosmopolitan in her right hand. "Would you mind, gentleman, if I borrowed Mister Ryan for a moment?" she said, with a broad smile, slightly tipsy. "I need him to settle an argument with the bartender about the proper ingredients of a mixed drink."

Both Cramden and Rudenko nodded.

As Ryan went off with her, the couple maintained a polite distance from one another and made a point not to reveal any other outward acknowledgements of their relationship. Even so, there were few on board the Station who didn't already know they were sleeping together.

Under the din of the crowded reception hall, Rachel leaned over to Ryan and whispered, "I need to see you later tonight."

"I wish I could."

"I could re-arrange the duty schedule so that I could meet you in your quarters sometime after midnight."

"We can't."

"We can't?" she repeated.

"All right, I can't."

"Or won't?"

Ryan paused for a moment to look at Rachel squarely in the face, but the look was only a fleeting one. Their words were low whispers, but to everyone pushing and moving around them in the reception hall, their exchange seemed very cordial, almost friendly, but not romantic.

"You surprise me," Ryan said.

"Well, you're the one full of surprises, aren't you?" she replied. "I travel half-way across the Solar System to be with you; we make love, and now all you want to do is avoid me."

"I made love to you last night and the night before because you're gorgeous, sexy, tempting and dangerous. And because I wanted to make love to you. What were you doing?"

Rachel was gravely silent. She was actually stunned by his words and couldn't think of a reply.

"Lobbying for the Jovian lifeforms?" he asked, then added, loud enough so that everyone around him could hear. "Without fresh cranberry juice, I'm afraid your Cosmopolitan is going to taste bitter."

Lenny appeared at their side, obviously sensing some tension between the two of them. The computer technician looked very different without his baseball cap and baggy pants. He put on the biggest smile. "That was a really inspiring speech, Mister Ryan," he said, then turned to Rachel, "There's a couple of people over here that I'd like you to meet."

He started to lead Rachel away from Ryan, but the blonde Science Officer kept her eyes on the man who had dared to insult her. A smile fluttered on her lips, then vanished as Ryan turned away to greet the delegates from Germany and France.

"Thanks so much for coming," he said, very practiced. "I really appreciate the support from your two nations."

16

In another part of the Space Station, the Communication's Center had been cleared of all civilians and Station personnel, and several large men in dark suits stood vigil near the entrance and beside the central imaging chamber, where holographic messages were received from and transmitted to Earth.

In a flurry of activity, Edward Reinhardt entered the Communications Center, escorted by several men. His familiar handkerchief was in hand and he kept using it to mop away the perspiration from his brow. He resembled a condemned man who was taking his last steps on the way to the gas chamber. When they reached the chamber, they released him and he stepped inside, completely of his own volition.

For the moment, Reinhardt was alone as the door closed behind him. The central imaging chamber was not unlike a phone booth, only considerably larger and more sophisticated. Overhead, a three-dimensional projector transmitted holographic images on a very narrow, subspace band which allowed for instantaneous communication with a person from Earth or one of the other colonies. He punched in several buttons on the main control panel in front of him, then took a step or two backwards from the prism that was the focal point of the image.

Suddenly, a ten-foot tall hologram of an attractive woman in her late forties materialized right before his eyes. Her image appeared almost ghost-like in the beam of light. She was very stylishly dressed in a black Armani suit, with a single row of white cultured pearls strung around her neck. In another time or place, she might have been mistaken for Hilary Clinton, the wife of the infamous twentieth-century President and the former Senator from New York. But she was, in fact, Susan Ryan, Mitchell's estranged wife and a political force in her own right.

"I told you that I had everything under control," Reinhardt said.

"Let's hope so," her quiet voice roared in the small chamber. "We can't afford to make any mistakes. Both of our lives are at stake here."

"You don't have to remind me of that. I've been dealing with men like these since well before you were born."

"Yes, but this is my show and my operation," Susan reminded him. "If anything goes wrong, it's my neck on the line, not yours."

"I told you I have everything under control. Nothing's going to go wrong."

"I wish I could believe that."

"Well, believe it!" he exclaimed, annoyed. "I've anticipated every possible scenario and made contingency plans for each."

"I expected no less," she said coldly. "You weren't exactly

brought into this for your sparkling personality, or for the fact that you are my father."

"Thanks."

"Don't mention it."

"Besides," Reinhardt added, "I've got a trump card...a person on the inside who is watching Ryan's every more. He can't take a crap without me knowing about it. If it looks like he's going to flip, I'll know about it before he does."

"Just make sure that you do."

Reinhardt and Susan exchanged knowing glances. Though they were father and daughter and related to one of the longest bloodlines in America, both knew there was no love lost between them.

"Susan, I don't expect to hear from you again until this is over," he said finally.

"It's always such a pleasure to talk with you, Edward."

Susan Ryan's ghost-like image suddenly disappeared from the beam of light in the central imaging chamber. Reinhardt did not move for an instant, then pulled out his familiar handkerchief and mopped his brow.

17

At about the same time, Yukiko Takahashi was working in the kitchenette of her two-bedroom living quarters. She had decided to skip the reception in order to spend some quality time with her son and mother-in-law. Besides, she was very much aware how unpopular her beliefs were with the current administration and felt that her presence at the affair might have been disruptive. And with Shibata opting to hold a twenty-four-hour vigil on the Mining Platform in order to gather much-needed data on the Jovians, she didn't even have a date to the party.

She had just stored the leftovers from dinner and was meticulously cleaning her dinnerware and putting them away in a storage cabinet. In the background, she heard the happy, carefree voices and music of an interactive George Lucas movie on the holographic projector in the living room, and smiled. Her son was watching his favorite film for the third time this week. She put away the last dish, closed and sealed the cabinet, and glanced up at the clock.

"Hiroki. Time for bed, my love," she said in Japanese.

She removed her apron and turned the corner to the living room where Hiroki was curled around the holographic unit, fast asleep. Suki was dozing peacefully on the sofa. She pulled a handy comforter over her mother-in-law, then gently gathered Hiroki into her arms. It wasn't as easy as it used to be; he was getting bigger every day, and that fact reminded her how much she really missed the time when he was just an infant. Carefully, she carried him into his bedroom and placed him gently onto the bed. As she did, Hiroki stirred, only vaguely aware of his mother's attention, as she tucked him in.

"I didn't hear how it ended," he said in Japanese.

"The young Jedi rescued the beautiful princess from the dark Sith lord, and they both lived happily ever after," she replied.

"That's not what happened?"

"Yes, my love," she reassured him. "Now you must go to sleep."

"I'm afraid that I'll have bad dreams again," he cried. "Could you stay with me for a while?"

"I'll be right here, my love. Now go to sleep."

"Okay. Good night, mommy."

"Good night."

She gave him a kiss good night, then he rolled over and

went to sleep. She continued to sit on the edge of the bed, just looking down at him for a long moment. Her eyes had that winsome, faraway look that only parents understood when they looked at their children with love and affection. But her look soon turned to a melancholy one. Hiroki was so much his father's son, the complete essence of her late husband distilled down to one perfect little replica. And even though he was conceived in her womb from the cloned DNA of the man who was lost on the first Jupiter probe, she loved Hiroki nonetheless...perhaps even more.

Yukiko laid down next to her son and put her arms around him. She missed her late husband more than she was willing to admit to herself or her mother-in-law. She gave up the struggle to hold back tears and started weeping, holding her son close to her.

18

Inside the mess hall, the party was still going strong.

Bradford had moved to the front of the room and was standing in front of a microphone next to where Station personnel had stretched a wide, red ribbon across a makeshift stage. He had one last duty to perform before he could retire for the night and it was an important one. Bradford had assembled the members of the press, who had been purposely excluded from the reception, near the front of the stage with their cameras and recording equipment. He had also just dispatched dozens of waiters with hundreds of glasses of champagne.

On cue, the lights dimmed and a crude spotlight illuminated him.

"Ladies and gentlemen," his voice echoed through the sound system, "I would like to call Mister Ryan back up to the stage for the highlight of this evening's festivities. The ceremonial cutting of the ribbon that will officially open this Station."

The mess hall thundered with applause as another spotlight captured Mitchell Ryan in a small circle of people at the back.

Ryan started to move forward, nodding to his guests and making his way toward the front of the room. He stopped to shake hands with a couple of friends, then continued walking. There was a murmur as Ryan's image suddenly appeared on all of the monitors, following him to the stage.

"Good evening," he said, first smiling into the cameras for the press, then looking out over the hall. "I want to thank you all for coming but, more importantly, I want to assure you that…I don't have another long speech."

The room broke out into laughter, followed by more applause.

Ryan relished it, especially after seeing Rachel in the company of that computer technician. She had told him, only a few hours before, that she had a date for the day's festivities and he had dismissed it without a second thought. He didn't view Lenny Provenzo as any kind of threat. But actually seeing them together, having fun at his inauguration, was something else entirely. For the first time in their twenty-year relationship, Ryan felt jealous.

"Tonight, we celebrate the opening of this new, state-of-the-art facility for mining the precious energy resources our home world needs," he continued, speaking into the microphone. "And I would like to dedicate it, not just to our children, or our children's children, but to the many generations that follow…"

The mess hall broke out into applause once again.

"Now, if I can coax Miss Jacqueline Johnston, the former Miss Universe, to come to the stage," Ryan said, smiling and looking off to his right, then left. "She will assist me with these final honors."

Jackie stepped forward, carrying a pair of large scissors with both hands. Miss Johnston was a tall, statuesque redhead with gleaming, white teeth and sparkling green eyes. She smiled and waved to the crowd, like she had done at a hundred other venues since being crowned at a beauty pageant in Miami Beach two years earlier. The room grew silent when she handed Ryan his half of the scissors. It was a dramatic moment. Bradford looked on with anticipation as they placed the scissors on the wide red ribbon and cut it. Simultaneously, there was a sudden jolt, like someone had stepped on the brakes and just as quickly released them. The Station swayed back and forth, and the lights flickered off, then on, and finally off again.

Everyone in the mess hall gasped or screamed. All of the monitors around the room blanked out, and the message: PLEASE STAND BY, appeared a moment later. All at once the emergency alarm sounded. Furious, Ryan looked around for a cut-off switch, but found himself distracted by the dozen or so people who had tossed aside their glasses of champagne and were bolting for exits. That action triggered several others to start searching for the exits, while still others had begun trooping obediently through a set of double doors into the corridor. He was afraid there would be a panic and stepped to the edge of the stage.

"Now, that's what I call a pretty potent drink," Ryan said in a loud, commanding voice, trying to allay the fears of all of his guests.

For a moment, his joke didn't register, but then, as it filtered through the crowd in the form of a repeating murmur, people started laughing. Not all at once, but in pockets that eventually filled the hall. With the laughter, the overhead lights felt obliged to come back on to life, and did, and the alarm was finally silenced.

Smiling, Ryan moved out among his guests, shook hands and exchanged pleasantries. The faint aura of edgy politeness had returned, but at least Ryan found it easier to handle with a few glasses of champagne. Out of the corner of his eye, he caught a glimpse of his mistress walking out the double doors with Provenzo. Rachel tried to suppress a smile.

19

As the herd of people clogged the entrance and the corridor just beyond, Rachel and her date merged with the crowd. Outside the mess hall, Bradford and his public relations staff had their hands full. They attempted to explain that the party was not over and that what had happened was a false alarm, but most of the guests and Station personnel had had enough for the night. They began lining up for the elevators, Rachel and Lenny among them.

"I had a really good time tonight," he said to her while they stood and waited for the next lift to arrive.

"I'm glad," she replied, looking away. "Thanks for accompanying me."

"You're really special, Rachel. You're the kind of girl that..."

Rachel slumped, feeling all of the weight of his emotional immaturity heaped on her back like a five-hundred pound valentine. She was certain that, if she had unlocked the door to his heart, she would have been buried in an avalanche of broken dreams and unfulfilled promises. She felt sorry for Lenny because he was such a sweet man; if only he'd learned a few social skills along the way, this would not have been so painfully hard. How could she respond to him without encouraging him further, or making herself seem like a total bitch?

"...I always thought would be right for me."

"Why, thank you, Lenny," she said at last. "You're special in your own way."

"I don't suppose we could go out again?"

"Sure," she replied, "but just as friends."

Lenny swallowed hard, remembering their last conversation. "I know, I know. You've got a boyfriend," he replied, fumbling for the right words. "I hope he appreciates you as much as I do."

Rachel nodded, noncommittally. "He tries."

Lenny looked puzzled for a moment and tried to bring to mind what she meant by her two-word statement. Did he detect a note of cynicism in the tone of her voice? A sense that she wasn't getting everything that she deserved? A desire for someone or something better? He shrugged broadly and turned to her with all of the warmth and charm that he could muster.

"Because if you were my girlfriend, you'd never have to do a thing. I'd take really good care of you."

"I'm sure that you would," she replied, smiling faintly.

He smiled wide back to her, his eyes dancing wildly.

"You're going to make some girl out there," Rachel added as the elevator arrived for them, "a very lucky woman."

"But I've already met..."

She quickly changed the subject. "Would you like a breath wafer?"

"Thank you," he said, taking one from her hand. "You know, I read somewhere that when a woman offers a man a breath wafer at the end of a date, that means she wants him to kiss her."

She took a deep breath and sighed.

"Does this mean we're going to kiss?"

"No, it's just a breath wafer. Nothing more!"

Lenny stopped talking. While the elevator groaned upward to their individual levels, the silence grew heavy between them.

At level ten, she walked out without a backwards glance. When the lift reached his floor, he stepped out, dejected and alone, and watched the doors close swiftly on his dream.

20

Several hundred kilometers below the Station, in the forward compartment of the Mining Platform, Masaki Shibata was dead. His body lay sprawled on the floor near the great circular window. His arms and legs were stretched out and his face was pressed to the Plexiglas. His mouth was covered with blood and white foam.

Above him, just on the other side of the window, Cloud Dancer watched and waited for Shibata to react, for he had been calling to him for a period of time only the Terrans would have counted as several hours. The Jovian lifeform did not understand why he failed to respond to his telepathic call. Cloud Dancer was devoid of any kind of expression or emotion, but he did convey a sense of confusion and frustration that only his fellow Jovians could comprehend.

In the sea of clouds, as far as the horizon, hundreds of them had paused, watching and waiting, similarly confused and similarly frustrated. They could not have known that he was dead, for they had no concept of mortality.

21

Ryan paced up and down the corridor outside Rachel's quarters, trying to summon the courage to knock on her door, but the longer he paced, the more he realized it just wasn't there. Only a few hours before, she begged to see him, but he had been so cruel, so thoroughly dismissive to her, that he was convinced she would slam the door in his face if he knocked. Or worse, she'd refuse to answer. And he just could not face her rejection now, even if it meant going back to his quarters alone. Ryan knew there would be no badges of courage for him this night, for all of the battles had been fought and all of his heroes had long since passed into memory.

He walked up to her door one final time, and paused.

All of a sudden, the door opened, and Rachel was waiting for him in the entrance, wearing a black evening gown that revealed all of the wonderful curves of her body. He dropped his jaw in shock.

"Do you mind telling me how much longer you intend on pacing outside of my quarters?" she asked, with a grin.

"How did you know?"

"I've been waiting for you.

Ryan shook his head. He was both pleased and a little annoyed to be so transparent to her. He lingered outside of her door for another moment, a grin forming on his face.

"You know, you remind me of a girl I dated in college before my wife."

"Really."

"She was very beautiful," he explained. "She also confused me. A lot."

Rachel's beautiful lips formed a lovely, beaming smile. She beckoned him into her quarters, then took him into her arms as he crossed the threshold. She leaned forward and kissed him. It was hesitant at first, but then she opened her mouth and kissed him deeply.

She whispered, "I hope you've come here to show me just how confused you really are."

He pulled her closer and kissed her again. Looking into

her blue eyes, he said, "I expect I can come up with something."

He reached behind her back and unzipped her dress. Her shoulders were bare, so he kissed them lightly as he cupped her breasts in each hand. Rachel moaned softly, then pulled him tightly against her. She had needed this all day long, and held onto him like life itself.

Just beyond their embrace, in the dark recesses of the corridor, the Shadow Man watched and waited.

Thursday

22

In the morning, Ryan was frantically searching Rachel's room for something he had misplaced during the night. He was partially dressed in a shirt and a tie and slacks, but he was still clearly missing parts of his wardrobe. He looked under her bed, then under her pillows and blankets, and finally under the see-through gown that was laying over her nightstand. But he still couldn't seem to find whatever it was that he was missing.

Meanwhile, Rachel was very calm and sedate. Dressed only in a matching black pair of bra and panties, she sat in front of her vanity mirror and continued to put on her make-up.

"I can't go to a meeting with the delegates from the United Planets this morning half naked," he stated.

"Then just don't go. We can stay in bed and order meals from your steward."

"Very funny."

"Are you sure you were wearing two socks when you came here last night?" she asked, with her tongue firmly planted in her cheek.

He paused briefly to consider her question. "Of course I was wearing two socks. I have two feet and I always put one on each foot when I get dressed in the morning."

"Really, is that something you learned from your wife, or did you just pick it up along the way?"

"Ha. Ha." Ryan acted like he was amused. "Now forget the makeup and just help me find my sock."

Rachel laughed, but continued applying her makeup. She had no intention of stopping what she was doing to help him look for his sock, and the expression of resolution on her face conveyed that feeling.

"If you find my sock for me, I'll reconsider my decision about the Jovians."

"That's not funny, Mitchell," she said angrily, turning from her vanity mirror to meet his gaze. "There are people who have put their lives, their entire careers on the line to protect those lifeforms. For them, it's not a laughing matter."

Ryan had given up his search. He sat down on the edge of the bed and pulled on his shoe without the sock. Then he stood up and adjusted his pant leg so that it wouldn't show.

"I'm sorry," he confessed.

"Well, maybe you don't realize just how important this is."

Ryan returned Rachel's gaze. He was about to say something more when the comlink attached to his belt chimed. He snapped it open, with a flick of his wrist, and brought it to his right ear.

"Ryan here."

Rachel could not hear the other part of the conversation, but as she watched Ryan's serious expression turn grim, she knew that something was wrong. He was visibly shaken by the news.

"Okay," he concluded the conversation. "I'll be there just as quickly as I can."

Ryan snapped the comlink shut and returned it to his belt.

He reached for his suit coat which was lying across the bed. He was deliberately avoiding eye contact with her.

"What's wrong?"

"Shibata's dead," he replied, barely able to say the words. "His body was just found on the Mining Platform."

"Oh, my God."

"I know the two of you didn't like one another, but as a favor to me, could you please let Doctor Takahashi know," he added, in a low whisper. "You'd better prepare her. I'm told it's not a pretty site."

Rachel nodded in disbelief, both hands holding her head in place so that it would not slip off her shoulders. She seemed unable to comprehend what she had just been told, and was visibly shaken by the news.

"I'm on my way there, now," Ryan said as he walked out the door.

23

Doctor Shibata's body was the first thing Ryan saw when he entered the forward observation chamber of the Mining Platform. The small, twenty by thirty-five foot compartment teemed with activity as members of Cramden's Security Team secured the room and members of Rudenko's medical staff put away their equipment, but all he could see was the body. Except for the blood on his mouth, Shibata looked rather peaceful. The former Senator thought there was something about the total lack of movement and expression that made his death seem all the more surreal. Like someone taking a quiet catnap under an elm tree at the park, Ryan kept waiting for him to wake up and start moving about, but he knew that would never happen. Less than four days before, he had been standing in that very room, conversing with him in Japanese, and now the eminent scientist was dead.

Ryan looked around the compartment and his eyes met Cramden's. "Lloyd," he said without emotion, "have you talked with the person who found the body?"

"Yes, I have," Cramden replied. "It was one of the maintenance engineers. She discovered the body during her early morning rounds and immediately called it in to her supervisor."

Ryan glanced at Rudenko. "What did he die of?"

"Well, that's really a question for the coroner," he responded, deferring to Doctor Deckers. "But if I had to guess, I'd say he choked to death." Rudenko pointed to the area around Shibata's mouth. "Take a look at his mouth. That's blood and tissue he coughed up from his lungs."

"Choked to death," Ryan repeated to himself.

At that moment, Yukiko rushed into the chamber, followed closely by Rachel. The diminutive Japanese scientist pushed her way through the crowd of onlookers, then fell to her knees next to the body. She gathered the lifeless form into her arms, like a small child clutching a rag doll, and started weeping.

"Oh, Masaki," she cried aloud.

Rachel approached the body with respect, her arms folded in front of her. She had tears in her eyes.

"Good God. How could he have choked to death?" Ryan asked.

"It's been know to happen to deep sea divers," Rachel replied. "If their mixture of gas is too rich in oxygen, the tremendous pressures of the deep make it far more lethal than cyanide."

Cramden and Rudenko drew nearer with quite natural curiosity, since neither of them had ever heard of such a thing. Neither had Ryan.

"Once he started breathing the air, the highly corrosive oxygen burned away the inner lining of his lungs," she continued, "and in a matter of minutes, Shibata was literally drowning in his own lung tissue." Rachel wiped away her tears. "Not a pleasant way to die."

"I concur," Rudenko said.

"So, what you're saying is that someone deliberately switched the mixture of gas for the Mining Platform?" Ryan asked her.

"Deliberately?" she replied, with a raised eyebrow. "I'm not sure if I would go that far. It could have been an accident."

Ryan shook his head. "Accidents don't happen twice. If what you are saying is true, then someone had to have switched the mixture twice. Otherwise, we'd all be lying next to Shibata. Dead."

"Yes, of course," Rachel said, the look of awareness slowly dawning on her face. "Whoever killed Masaki switched the mixture back, after he was dead, so that the maintenance workers could discover the body."

"Any indication of foul play?" Ryan asked his Security Chief.

"None, whatsoever," Cramden responded. "The log book indicates that he was alone on the Platform. No one came up or went down until after the maintenance crew arrived early this morning."

"This is damned peculiar," the former Senator said to himself.

Takahashi glared at Ryan sharply, as though surprised and yet totally certain of her suspicions. She had overheard the exchange between Ryan and his staff, and her eyes were full of rage.

"You killed him," her voice said from behind them.

"No, Yukiko..." Rachel said, turning around to her. "You don't know what you're saying. Ryan was with me last night."

Discreetly, Cramden nodded to Rudenko, but before her revelation could sink into the Chief Medical Officer's thoughts, Takahashi was on her feet, nose to nose with Ryan, staring him down.

"I know exactly what I am saying," she replied. "Masaki risked his life to prove the findings you dismissed."

Rachel tugged at her arm. "We've all taken those risks, Yukiko."

"You alone are responsible for his death," she said to Ryan.

"Doctor Takahashi, I am truly sorry for your loss, but we all take risks. That's the nature of our work here," he stated, without any emotion. "Doctor Shibata knew that. And it's about time you started realizing that this project is bigger and more important than any one man."

Yukiko slapped him across the face with the palm of her hand. "Masaki Shibata was more of a man than you will ever be."

Rachel and the others reacted to the slap, but Ryan did not flinch. Instead, he stared at the diminutive Japanese scientist with deep penetrating eyes, then turned to Rudenko.

"Please see that Doctor Deckers conducts a complete autopsy of the body," he requested. "I must return to the Station immediately."

But before Rudenko could reply, Ryan had already turned and was walking out of the compartment.

24

"There's a dead man at my mining site," Ryan shouted, barging into the elegant, exclusive Presidential Suite that overlooked the Station's Central Core, "and that makes me very angry."

Reinhardt stepped out of the toilet facility, a straight razor in his left hand and shaving cream partially covering the right side of his face.

"Come in," he said, both startled and amused. "I guess I should have someone come up and check that lock. I wouldn't want to have just anyone barging in here."

"I said there's a dead man at..."

"Yes, yes, I heard you," he replied, returning to the marble basin in the adjoining room. "Shibata...that was an unfortunate accident. Takahashi was the real target."

"Unfortunate," Ryan repeated, and followed after the old man. "Is that all you've got to say? Unfortunate. We're not talking about some dumb animal that ran out in front of a speeding truck."

Reinhardt continued shaving, moving the razor across his face with slow, determined strokes, listening, but more concerned with his shave. When he finished, the seventy year-old reached into the basin and splashed a handful of water into his face. He straightened up as far as he could, revealing stiffness in his lower back, and reached for a plush red towel.

Ryan's eyes narrowed as he studied the other man's wrinkled features. They were cool and unflappable. "This doesn't seem to bother you."

"No, Mitch, it doesn't bother me," he said, wiping his face once with the towel, then tossing it carelessly across the room into the shower stall. "What does bother me is your reaction to it."

"Am I supposed to be grateful?"

"For a start," Reinhardt returned.

Ryan shook his head. He seemed at a complete loss for words, not that it mattered. He felt like nothing he said made a difference.

He hurried across the room, opened the sliding glass door and stepped onto the balcony for a breath of fresh air. "Did I just stumble into some alternate reality?" Ryan asked, his voice full of irony. "How many years did I listen to you tell me that one of the things that separated us from those soulless terrorists on Mars was the value we placed on human life?"

"Yes, I do recall saying that," he answered with a slight shrug. "But I also remember telling you that sometimes the ends justified the means." Reinhardt pulled on a white, button-down shirt. "The fact remains is that what we're doing here is a very important and necessary part of our efforts to maintain our way of life, and if a few people have to be sacrificed for the greater good, then so be it."

"I doubt seriously if Shibata would have agreed with you."

"Well, then, he never really saw the view from the top."

Ryan leaned over the suite's narrow balcony to take in the cycloramic view of the Station's Central Core. The sight was breathtaking, even to someone who had just stared into the great eye of Jupiter. He watched the hang-gliders weaving back and forth, then looked down to see people the size of ants moving along various ramps and platforms far beneath him. The warm air from the reactor below swept against his face, and, for a moment, he forgot where he was. But only for a moment.

"I take that back," he said, putting his thumb close to one eye and squinting to remove one of the people below from his line of sight. "Shibata wasn't some dumb animal caught in the headlights. He was an ant, and you stuck your thumb out and squashed him."

Reinhardt hid his smile and managed a look of disdain instead. "You just don't understand, do you? Perhaps, in time, you'll see things in a different light."

Ryan drew himself together and the determined look settled back on his face. "Now, I want to show you something," he said, returning to the room and putting a hand under the other man's elbow. He tugged firmly on Reinhardt's arm, and the seventy year-old reluctantly accompanied him to the balcony. "I want to show you what the view from the top really looks like."

"I don't like heights," Reinhardt said, struggling to break free.

Ryan maintained his grasp and pressed the old man's upper body to the railing. "Well, then, by all means, you should take a look."

"Mitchell!"

"Take a really good look," he repeated, forcing him nearly over the edge.

"Mitchell, have you lost your mind!"

"I could throw you over this railing just as easily as you killed Shibata," he scowled, pushing him closer to his doom. "But I didn't take this post to become partners with you in murder."

Reinhardt's legs began to buckle and his breathing was hard and labored.

"And this is never going to happen again," Ryan added. "Right?"

Reinhardt was gravely silent.

"Am I right?" Ryan demanded. When he realized that he wasn't going to get one, he simply loosened his grip and stepped aside.

Reinhardt scrambled backwards until he reached the safety of his room, then collapsed to the floor, clutching his chest. His breathing continued to be hard and labored, and sweat was dripping from his forehead. The wrinkles on his face had flattened out into a frightful death's-head. But he still managed the smile of a man who had looked into the abyss, and had lived to boast about it.

"No more murders, no more accidents," Ryan explained. "Or you'll be the next one they find dead."

Ryan turned and walked to the open door. He hoped he had made his message clear to Reinhardt. He wasn't a killer, but if pressed, he felt like he was capable of anything.

Ryan stormed out of the suite and down the hall. Hidden from him in the darkness, the Shadow Man watched and waited.

25

Rumors of Shibata's death had spread throughout the Station like wildfire, but the only truth, if one could call it that, lay in the official Coroner's report on the Chief Administrator's desk. Ryan glanced through the last few pages of the report, then tossed it across his oak-wood desk to Doctor Deckers who stood at attention on the other side. A short man with a medium build, nondescript features and thinning hair, Deckers was the kind of individual who would have been overlooked at parties and other social gatherings had it not been for the smell of formaldehyde. He had spent the years since medical school, drifting from one undistinguished post to another, blending into the background like forgotten furniture.

"Well, have you completed the blood work, or not?" Ryan asked.

"Of course I have," the Coroner replied.

"And?

"And what?"

Ryan looked around his office, irritated. Strips of light from the low ceiling bounced off his shiny oak desk.

"Doctor Deckers, I'm not taking a survey," he said, the intonation of the words revealing his growing impatience. "If you did the analysis, I'd like to know the results of the blood work."

"Nothing conclusive."

"What about the tissue sample from his damaged lungs?"

"If you look carefully at the last page of my report, you'll find the answers," Deckers replied, returning the report to him.

Ryan studied the stack of papers. He stopped at the last

sheet and read through the data. "I don't understand," he revealed. "If this report is correct, then what you're telling me is that Shibata's lungs just gave out. He died of natural causes. This can't be correct."

"It is correct."

Ryan took another look at the report and frowned.

"What about the poison toxins from the gas mixture?"

"I found no evidence of poisoning."

Ryan put the report down and leaned over his desk, examining Deckers from head to foot.

"What's going on here?"

"What do you mean?"

"Look," he said, shaking the index finger of his right hand at Deckers, "I may not have been the most honest politician that ever held office, but I can tell when I'm being lied to. Who told you to falsify this report?"

"I don't know what you're talking about."

"If my Science Officer said Shibata was poisoned by some odd mixture of gases, then you can bet your reputation that he was."

"I found no evidence of poisoning," he said, defending his report.

"You're not a very convincing liar, Doctor."

"Mister Ryan...if I may speak frankly..."

"Did you also falsify the report about Bennett's death?"

"...you're out of line."

"Get the Hell out of my office!" the Chief Administrator exploded, pointing Deckers at the door. "Go back and tell Reinhardt that it won't work. I see right through his sordid little plans."

Ryan wadded up the report in his hand and threw it across the room, narrowly missing the Coroner as he propelled himself out the door. Things were starting to make sense, and that's what frightened him.

26

Reinhardt was alone in the central imaging chamber, with the phantom image of Susan Ryan shimmering in a beam of bright light before him. Actually, because of the unique way the imaging prism caught the light, she towered over him like a schoolmaster at an English boarding school. He wondered if she was going to admonish him with words, or simply crack him on the head with a yardstick. Reinhardt wiped the sweat from his brow, then tucked his handkerchief safely away in the pocket of his trousers. He had finally summoned the courage to speak.

"What's the problem, Susan?"

"Ryan."

"I'll handle him."

"Doesn't look like you're doing a very good job."

"I said I'd handle it," Reinhardt said, annoyed. "I've been handling him for years. I know his weaknesses."

"I know his weaknesses, too. Remember that I was married to him for twenty-five years."

"But I was always better at handling him than you were."

Susan Ryan took a deep sigh. "They're pretty upset about this, Edward. I wouldn't be calling you myself if they weren't."

"They're overreacting."

"Well, they don't think so."

"What do they want me to do?"

"Get rid of him."

"Get rid of Ryan? I can't, not without raising a lot of suspicion. And as it is, there's already some suspicion about Bennett's death."

"Do it," Susan said coldly.

"No."

"The feeling's very strong about this, Edward."

Reinhardt and Susan looked at each other with contempt, like two stags locked by their antlers in a life and death struggle for survival. He reached up to jab Susan with his right fist, and her holographic image winked out temporarily and then, just as fast, came back into focus.

"I said that I would take care of it, and I will take care of it," Reinhardt said finally. "The mining operation will start as planned, and you can assure all of your investors of that."

"Don't disappoint me on this," she said, pointing at him. "Because the next time I call, they'll be no pretense of civility, and I won't be talking to you as your daughter. I'll be calling you to read your obituary."

"I'm glad we had this chance to talk."

Susan Ryan nodded her head determinedly, then her ten-foot-tall holographic image disappeared into the prism. Reinhardt breathed a deep sign of relief as he pulled the hand-kerchief across his perspiring brow.

27

Rachel finished washing her hair and wrapped it in a towel. She slipped on one of the terry-cloth robes that Ryan liked to have for his sleepovers, and rubbed the pile of absorbent fabric up and down trying very hard to imagine herself in his arms. Now she regretted that she hadn't made more of an effort to pull him away from his work. Rachel didn't want to admit it to herself, but she really needed Ryan, and missed him every time he wasn't there.

She moved into the living room of her quarters, ready to settle down and catch up on reading the news dispatches from Earth, when there came a light tap on the door. She smiled know-ingly, and untied the knot in her robe.

Rachel opened the door, saying, "Well, I'm really pleased…"

Her heart leaped into her throat. Lenny was standing at the entrance, wearing his baseball cap and baggy pants. She immediately pulled her robe closed and tried to slam the door in his face, but his fingers got in the way. He yelped like an animal that had gotten its paw snared in a trap, but still managed to pull his fingers free. She finally closed the door and stood with her back to it, shaking and trying to regain her composure.

"Rachel," Lenny said sheepishly from the other side, "I don't suppose I could talk with you for a minute."

"It's kind of late, Lenny," she replied. "Can't it wait until morning?"

"No, I'm sorry. This really can't wait."

"Okay, just give me a minute," she said, her hands shaking. She pulled her robe tight and tied the knot several times. She shook her head out of the towel and raked her fingers back through the knotted ends of her blonde hair. Still flushed, she opened the door.

He entered her room, licking the beads of blood off his knuckles like a child licking wayward drops of maple syrup. She saw the pained look on his face.

"Lenny, you're bleeding. Let me get you a towel," she cried, scurrying into the bathroom. She came back out with a wet hand towel and some bandages. "I'm really sorry. I thought you were someone else and I guess I just panicked."

"That's okay. It just looks worse than it is. Please don't bother…" he started to say, but before he could get the words out of his mouth, she was already plying him with care.

Rachel dabbed the blood away with the cold, wet hand towel, then carefully wrapped a bandage around his bruised hand. He contorted his face in pain, but she was pretty sure none of his fingers were broken. The muscles and joints would most likely be sore, but she was convinced that he'd survive.

"What's so important that it couldn't wait until morning?" she asked, at last.

"I've been working on that theory of ours," he replied, taking off his baseball cap and making himself comfortable on her couch. "I'm now certain the Jovians have been trying to communicate with us using electrostatic discharges in the same way neurons in our brain communicate with each other, and with the other cells of the body, through electric pulses."

"You came here to tell me that," she said, with one hand on her hip and the other one angling to the door. "Well, you can just get the…"

"No, no, wait, there's more," he said, leaning forward, the palms of both hands raised defensively in front of him. "When I correlated the data of the lightning strikes with all of the other factors, I discovered an interesting coincidence."

Rachel glared at him.

"Each time, the voltage meter of the shield generator recorded a hit, Doctor Shibata was the only scientist on duty at the Platform."

For an instant, she considered his words dispassionately as an interesting intellectual exercise, then a strange expression came over her face. The solution had been in front of them the whole time. "The Jovian lifeforms were communicating with Shibata," she concluded.

"Exactly!" he exclaimed, nearly jumping out of his seat. "I did some more checking, and discovered that, on the day when he was murdered, the Platform was struck by lightning six times, more than at any one time in the past. And since his death, no additional strikes have been recorded."

She raised one eyebrow, brooding. "The Jovians are probably confused right now," she said, thinking aloud. "They don't know why he stopped communicating with them. They don't know if he's angry, or confused, or disinterested, or just away taking a long nap."

"How do we tell them he's dead?"

"Well, if the Jovians regard the Mining Platform as some kind of living thing, not unlike themselves, then they see Shibata as the brain center. I don't think it would be advisable to tell them the brain is dead."

"Okay, if that's true, then how do *we* talk to them?"

"I don't know," Rachel replied with a shrug. "Humans rely almost entirely on words and gestures for communication, and yet even between the different cultures and nations on Earth, we still have great deal of difficulty understanding each other. We've never been able to talk with dolphins or whales or primates. For many years, we thought that we could use gestures and other visual clues to communicate with them because they were, after all, mammals like us, with a similar genetic makeup. But today, they're still just as alien to us as we are to them. I don't know how we could possibly even begin to bridge that gap with the Jovians."

"If only we had a universal translator…" Lenny mused, making an obscure reference to a television show that was over a hundred years old.

"I had you pegged as a 'Star Trek' geek," she said with a bemused look, finally sitting down next to him.

"Science fiction fan," he corrected her. Science fiction fans had actually become recognized as a religious minority group, like Baptists or Transgenders, the decade before Lenny was born. When others his own age were studying the teachings of Christ or Marx, he read the works of Clarke and Heinlein. One hundred years earlier, he would have been one of a few hundred misfits who were forced to cloister themselves in small, out of the way hotels to discuss the esoteric doctrines of Grokking, Vulcan mysticism and the Force, in order to avoid intolerance and persecution. But now, on the weekend retreats when he entered the temple of Asimov, Lenny and others like him had the freedom to worship as they liked without fear of ridicule.

"I've seen some of the old science fiction movies that were holographed."

"Remember the one when aliens come to Earth pretending to be our friends and accidentally leave behind a book titled 'To Serve Man,' and it turns out to be a cookbook?" he asked, barely able to contain his excitement.

"That was always one of my favorites," Rachel lied.

"What were those aliens called?" he asked rhetorically scouring his mind for that ancient piece of esoteric trivia, and then, just as quickly as it came to him, blurting it out: "Kanamits. That's right. They were called Kanamits."

"I don't think the Jovians intend to eat us."

"No, no, that's not my point," he protested. "In all of those old movies, the aliens always spoke perfect English. Not only did they know our words and phrases, but they also demonstrated an understanding of our grammar, syntax, idioms, inflections and so on. Even in the ones where they spoke stilted or broken English, they could still put together rudimentary subject-predicate statements."

"Is there a point here?" she asked, growing weary.

"My point is that the aliens in most of those movies learned to speak our language by first communicating with us telepathically."

"With all due respects to your religious beliefs, Lenny, that was science fiction. This is reality."

"Reality is a crutch for those people who can't handle science fiction."

Rachel took a deep breath and sighed. "Only human arrogance would assume the Jovians are going to float right up, and say in stilted English, 'Take me to your leader,' because they pulled it out of Shibata's brain."

"I disagree," he said, thinking. "Every form of intelligence develops symbol-systems for representing objects, causes and goals, and for formulating and remembering the procedures it develops for achieving those goals. An alien intelligence should have little difficulty assimilating those symbol-systems."

"I've heard that argument before," she said, rubbing her eyes. "That's what the scientists and researchers told us they were doing with cetacean life, but I don't think teaching a few tricks to dolphins and killer whales held in captivity necessarily proves their hypothesis."

"Well, it worked, didn't it? Didn't they show that it was possible to communicate with another species through objects and symbols?"

"Not necessarily," Rachel objected. "Humans tend to break things down as cause and effect, noun and verb, action and reaction because we are so goal-oriented. We like to see the progression of steps from point A to point B. But an alien species might well perceive entire scenes as a whole instead of breaking them down into clumsy things with properties? The Jovians might see the real world as steady flow of formless space in time, instead of separate, arbitrary man-made fragments, which are themselves approximations of reality, and not reality itself."

"Plato's allegory of the cave?"

"Exactly. We often mistake our own reality for the highest level of reality because we experience it through our five senses, which can be fallible. But this is merely a perceived reality, and not the truest of all realities. The Jovians may have the ability to experience reality in its truest form and, if so, their alien minds may be hardwired in an entirely different way from ours. Communication may not be possible in the manner that we have come to expect."

Lenny was grinning from ear to ear. A beautiful woman with brains, he thought to himself.

"I will concede that we are dealing here with something totally different," he said, then added, "but I still think the Jovians will rely on some form of telepathy to learn our language and the way we think."

"*Klaatu barada nikto*," Rachel replied.

Lenny looked at her with astonishment. "That's one of our high holy phrases! How did you know it?"

She shrugged, rising to her feet. "I seem to remember it from one of those old movies I saw on hologram."

"The more I get to know about you…"

"Lenny, it's rather late," she interjected, and ushered him to the door. "We should both try to get a good night's rest."

"Yeah, you're right," he said, dejected. He snapped the baseball cap back on his head and moved towards the door. "I'm going to try running some simulations through the Station's mainframe tomorrow. Maybe I can figure out an algorithm of the frequency modulation for the electrostatic discharges."

"Lenny, if anybody can crack this, you can."

"Thanks for saying that, Rachel, but aren't you giving me more credit than I deserve?"

"No, I'm not," she said, leaning forward to reassure him with a touch of her hand to his chest. "Deep inside here, where it counts, you have this amazing drive to find the truth in all things, and I suppose that I'm a bit envious."

He took her hand in his and looked deeply into her eyes. The brim of his baseball cap brushed embarrassingly close to her forehead. "No, you're the one who's so amazing…"

"Why thank you," she said, again cutting him off short of a marriage proposal or some other inappropriate action. Rachel shook free of his grasp and opened the door for him. "Well…good night."

Deflated, the life drained completely out of his body, Lenny staggered towards the door like a zombie from a low-budget horror film. "Rachel, there's just one thing that still bothers me," he said over his shoulder.

"And what is that?"

"If Shibata was communicating with the Jovian lifeforms, then why didn't he tell anybody?"

"Maybe he did," she replied, "and they just didn't believe him."

Lenny bobbed his head. "Good night, Rachel."

"Good night, Lenny," she said at last, closing the door behind him. She leaned back against the door and pondered his question. Rachel Westin would spend the rest of the night thinking about it.

28

Ryan had already worked right through dinner and was likely to go on working right through the night. He sat behind his oak desk, weary and exhausted from the dozens of reports he had forced himself to analyze because he trusted few people with the responsibility. His rational mind was spinning out of control from all of the inconsistencies, and he rubbed the temples of forehead to relieve the tension. Perhaps, if he could close his eyes for a few minutes, he might feel energized enough to finish? But as he settled back in his chair for a short catnap, that's when he heard it....

"Dad," the voice in the shadows whispered, "We miss you."

Ryan awoke, startled. He looked around the room with annoyance to find that it was still empty, the way that he had left it mere moments before when he decided to take a nap. He thought he had heard someone whisper to him. Perhaps he was dreaming, but then again, it seemed very real.

"Charlie," he spoke into the intercom on his desk. "Did you just call for me?"

But there was no reply from the outer office. He recalled that Bradford had gone off duty four hours earlier, and that no one had been assigned to replace him at his duty station. Ryan surveyed the room again, then, satisfied, he settled back into his chair for another stab at forty winks.

Almost, as soon as he had closed his eyes, he heard it again.

"You've been away for so long, dad," another voice echoed in the darkness.

"What? Who's there?" Ryan called out, responding to what he thought was the voice of his son, but could not possibly be. His son was a billion miles away on Earth, attending college; both of them were. He had had enough of this practical joke, and was tired of playing the fool. One of his staff must have cooked up this practical joke; only it was no longer funny.

"Okay, whoever you are," he said aloud, "show yourself."

Just then...he felt a prickling sensation run down the center of his back. Very slowly, indeed reluctantly, he swung his swivel chair around, away from his desk and the connecting door to the outer office, toward the wall where his predecessor had hung various paintings of Earth. He had meant to take them down in order to hang pictures of his own, but his busy schedule soon made it less of a priority. In that very instant he wished that he had, for the one pastoral painting, which featured a peaceful, almost idyllic rendering of a house nestled among autumnal trees at sunset, started to come to life before his very eyes. He didn't know if he was dreaming or hallucinating, but he went with it.

An intense beam of light from the oil-on-canvas sunset pierced through the image and began to widen and flatten out in all directions of the room. Then particles of dust that had not been captured by the Station's air-filtration system started to dance into odd shapes and patterns before him, finally coalescing into familiar forms. At first, they were like crude clay figures modeled in the shape of men, then they were his two sons playing catch football, happily, without a care in the world. Tom was seventeen again, and still had the strong, muscular build befitting the captain of the football team; and Bill was fifteen again, lean and agile, forever the younger brother.

The beam continued to sweep over the room, like a gentle wave rolling onto the shore, transforming the cold, gray bulkheads into a crisp, fall afternoon. When the blinding white light finally reached Ryan, he instinctively tried to pull away, but it also swept over him.

Without surprise—and almost without fear—Ryan raised his hands slowly to his face and then looked down at himself; he was suddenly five years younger. He was also no longer sitting in his office, but was standing on the paved walkway to his home in Hunt Valley, Maryland. He remembered that moment from the past with fondness. On that particular day, Ryan had just returned from an economic summit on the Moon, and he was dead tired from the long flight. But the site of his sons playing catch football in the backyard made him feel very happy and helped to elevate his spirits.

Mitchell Ryan dropped his bags near the gate and leaned over the fence to watch them play. Tom was remarkably fit and tended to favor him with the stocky appearance and commanding presence; Bill was thinner, but he was extremely handsome and when he spoke, others listened. He was proud of them, but for very different reasons. Tom was a natural born leader; Bill was the scholar. How he had managed to raise two, such incredible sons was more a question his ex-wife could answer than he, for Ryan had spent far too many years away from them to take any credit.

The boys finally noticed him and came running over.

"Hey, dad, you're home," Tom shouted.

"We've really missed you, pop," Bill exclaimed.

"I have missed both of you," he said, reaching over the fence and pulling them into his embrace. "Besides, you didn't think I was going to miss the big homecoming game, did you? Not with Tom starting."

Ryan heard himself speaking the words and felt himself going through the motions, but he was somehow detached from the primacy of the moment as if he was an actor following the script of someone else's life. He tried to make some sense of where he was, but just ended up even more confused than before. Not only was he experiencing the moment again, but he was also viewing it as an observer. Ironically, he was the boy who went to the dance *and* the boy standing outside the window, looking in, wishing that he had gone to the dance.

"Where'd you go this time, dad?" Tom asked.

"Yeah, what were you doing?" Bill inquired.

"Well…" he struggled to deviate from the script the past had written for him by improvising his own dialogue, but the words came out of his mouth just as they had done once before. "…I had to attend an economic conference on Lunar One."

"Wow, you went to the moon," Tom said, with a twinkle in his eye. "I'd love to go with you sometime, dad."

"Me, too."

"Soon as the summer comes," he said, without volition.

"Promise?" Bill asked.

"You and Tom and I," Ryan said, the proud father. "I'll show you the first colony we built there. The Moon is full of beautiful cities and hardworking men and women, but Lunar One is my favorite place." He wanted to shed a tear of regret for that lost moment in time, but could control his tear ducts. "With the lower lunar gravity, they have a form of football there that you just wouldn't believe."

"Wow, I'll bet I could throw the football a mile on the Moon," Tom boasted, pumping the ball in his hand and snapping it off to his brother.

"You bet," Bill echoed, easily catching the pass and tucking it safely under his arm. He put his hand out in front of him and started running down the length of the yard like it was a football field. When he reached the fence, Bill turned around and ran back. "And I could run it into the goal without breaking a sweat."

Ryan smiled. "I see you've been practicing your downfield maneuvers," he said to Bill, then turned to Tom. "And you've been practicing your pass. I can tell that you're ready for the big game."

"I sure am," Tom replied, "Especially if you're gonna be there."

"What do they say about you in school, now that you've made captain?"

"There's a crowd of girls behind him every time the classes change," Bill reported, teasing his brother. The two boys tussled playfully with each other, then Tom came up with the ball.

"This Saturday, dad, this Saturday…just for you, I'm going to break through for a touchdown," he said.

"You're supposed to pass," Bill reminded him.

"I'm doin' one play for dad. You watch me, dad, and when I pat the top of my helmet, that means I'm breakin' out," he added, going through the motions. "Then you watch me crash through that line!"

Mitchell Ryan was almost in tears, for he remembered that day like it was yesterday, but he could not cry. His son Tom ran fifty-one yards and scored the winning touchdown for Marist High School. They gave him the game ball, and Tom was the toast of all the homecoming celebrations. It was one of the proudest moments of Ryan's life as a father, and he smiled, thinking, remembering his boys.

"We miss you, dad," he heard them calling to him as if far away.

When Ryan looked again, the phantom images were gone and he was sitting in his swivel chair, alone in the office. He didn't believe in ghosts, but knew that something truly wondrous had just happened. Had he been dreaming, or had the images of some past memory come to haunt him, like some Charles Dickens fable.

He looked back down at his desk and began working again.

29

Yukiko Takahashi found herself sleepwalking on the streets of New Tokyo. Even though her rational mind told her that she was still laying in the bed with her son Hiroki, the sights and sounds of the great metropolis that completely enveloped her on all sides fooled her into thinking that she was some place else. She walked calmly out of the metro station where she had just stepped off the bullet train from Osaka, the ancestral home of her noble family, and headed for the Marriott Marquis hotel where her husband Hiroki was staying.

Yukiko remembered the day like it was yesterday, and found it kind of odd going through the same paces again, like a digital recording that had been snapped back to a certain starting place and replayed. She felt her heart beating, her lungs pumping oxygen, her visual and audio senses responding, her arms swaying at her sides, and her legs moving, but she did not feel like she had any kind of control over her body. Had she wanted to stop or turn around and go back, she found herself incapable of transmitting the proper commands to her central nervous system. The Japanese scientist tried to make some sense of what was happening to her, but none of the hypotheses she formulated had enough data to reach a logical conclusion. She realized that all she could do was go along for the ride.

Without any volition of her own, Yukiko made her way up to his suite. She heard a voice inside and wasn't able to place it. She knocked firmly on the door, but there was no answer. Strange, she thought to the self that was merely observing. For the first time, since this playback of the past had begun, events were unspooling differently. In her remembrance of that particular day, Hiroki was supposed to greet her at the door with the news that he had been selected for the mission to Jupiter.

But on this run-through, when she knocked, he failed to answer it. Had her mind simply remembered the incident in different way? Or were two or more incidents being merged together into one? And why? She knocked again. Still no answer.

She opened the door carefully.

The holographic television was on in the front room accounting for the voice she had heard. Aki Wakabayashi was behind the anchor desk on CNN, reporting in Japanese, "…and appeals from the United Planets Security Council to the terrorist factions have had no calming effect on the Martian colonists who face the senseless violence on a daily basis at their homes on the red planet. Now, this just in…"

"Hiroki?" she called, looking through the suite.

She was about to click off the holographic television when Aki Wakabayashi continued, "…at 14:55 Earth Standard Time, the *Explorer II* airship, with two crew members aboard, was lost on an exploratory probe of the planet Jupiter. Reports from the *Vigilant*, which remains in orbit around the gas giant, indicate that all systems were go and that the two astronauts were in good spirits just moments before contact was broken. While it may never be possible to determine exactly what happened to the craft, all early indicators seem to point to an apparent malfunction in its electrical systems. At this hour, all attempts at a rescue have been discontinued, and the crew is being listed officially as missing, presumed dead. Our deepest sympathies go out to the families of Scott Glenn and Hiroki Takahashi, who now join a growing list of astronauts and cosmonauts who have died while…"

Her heart raced. She remembered hearing the news about Hiroki's death on the holographic simulcast in Osaka; the news report had been the same, but this was not how it had happened. How could she ever forget the pain and anguish of that single moment that defined her life? She recalled that she had been enjoying a visit with her parents when the simulcast began. No one from the Unified Space Agency had bothered to contact her in advance, so the news came as quite a shock. She spent the first three days in tears, crying for her dead husband, and on the fourth day, she used her new found status as a celebrity to wrangle a spot on the next survey expedition. But all of that had happened differently from this rendition of reality. Who or what was manipulating the events of her life, and to what purpose?

Yukiko continued her exploration of the suite, stepping into the bedroom where a second holographic television was broadcasting the news. The sound echoed throughout the hotel suite.

Even before she reached the center of the room, she saw her husband's body lying motionless on the bed. She raised her hands up to stifle the scream of terror that had been building inside her, and that was when she realized she had performed the first voluntarily action that had not been choreographed. The observer and the actor were merging back into one.

She started moving closer to confirm that he was dead, then froze in her steps, reluctant to go any further. Feelings of fear, grief, desperation, loneliness, shock—the myriad of emotions that she had felt these last fifteen years—were welling up in misery deep and genuine within her. She never should have allowed him to go on that mission. Until the time of launch, Yukiko had merely suspected that something was going to go wrong. But after the rocket blasted off for the International Space Station on the first leg of its eighteen-month journey to Jupiter, she was absolutely certain that she would never again see her husband. She cursed herself for letting him go; of course, there was nothing that she could have done to prevent him. Yukiko had thought about lying and telling him that she was pregnant, but realized how unforgivable that would have been. In the end, she simply hugged and kissed him goodbye.

She looked down at the figure on the bed and pondered

what she should do next. Part of her wanted to go over to it, and if it was indeed the body of her husband and not some ghostly phantom from her deepest fears, embrace him one final time. But the other part of her—the rational part—doubted the input of her own senses and made her question how any of this was possible. First, she wondered how she had managed to return to Earth, and why she was experiencing a collage of images from her past, including ones that had never happened. Then she looked over at the bed, and questioned how that could be him. Hiroki had died nearly a billion miles away from Earth. His body was never recovered, and as far as the government was concerned, he was still officially listed as missing in action, presumed dead.

Was she hallucinating this alternate reality? Was this all a dream, some nightmare dredged up from her subconscious mind?

Her confusion turned to tears and she began to sob. She could not help herself. Somewhere in the back of her mind she knew that this was all some kind of fantastic illusion, but she could not stop from going to his side.

With a heavy heart, she leaned over and kissed him lightly on the lips, and as she did, the figure was transformed into her son Hiroki. She reeled back in horror. All at once the scene changed, with the posh, elegant surroundings of the suite melting into the drab four walls of her quarters aboard the Station. The transition caught her leaning over her son. She was now standing next to her son's bed, looking into little Hiroki's angelic face as he slept peacefully.

After a moment of hesitation, she climbed onto the bed and pulled the covers back to snuggle next to her son. Her body was trembling and her hands shook as she pulled the sleeping child into her embrace. She continued crying right on through the night until morning.

Friday

30

Ryan sat at his desk with the Coroner's report on his predecessor's death, and realized that there was a connection, beyond the obvious, that linked Deckers to both murders, but he just could not make out what it was. He glanced over at the autopsy report on Shibata and shrugged. The Chief Administrator pushed both reports away and sat back watching the steam rise from his hot cup. He debated whether he should drink his morning's worth of caffeina or simply inject it into his veins. The milky-white alkaloid had replaced coffee as the stimulant of choice aboard the Station because of the Martian blockade, but it had not improved on the flavor. It still tasted bitter to him, but what he really missed more than coffee was the couple of lumps of sugar he used to sweeten the taste; they were was also on the embargo list.

Ryan took a couple of sips, frowned, then pulled Bennett's autopsy report back to him. He had already been up for over thirty-six hours, and had the suspicious feeling that it was going to be another one of those days. He was also having trouble shaking the vivid detail of the dream that he had experienced the night before, if it had been a dream.

A sudden commotion in his outer office confirmed that suspicion.

"Charlie, what the hell is going on out there?" he shouted at the door.

"Wait a minute! You can't go barging in there," Ryan heard his administrative aide cry out from the other side of the door, and all at once, both Bradford and Takahasi were standing in front of him.

"I'm sorry, Mister Ryan," Bradford apologized. "I told her you were busy. She just kinda got by me."

"Thanks a lot, Charlie," Ryan groaned inwardly. "If I need any more of your help, I'll send for you."

"Yes, sir," Bradford replied, turning and closing the door behind him.

"Doctor Takahashi, I'm a very busy man," Ryan said without a formal greeting. "What can I do for you?"

"I know you killed Masaki," she said with a distinct lisp, the words tumbling out of her mouth in an almost unintelligible manner.

"Now, hold it right there," Ryan objected. "If you're going to insult me…"

"You are the one who insults me with your lies. You are the one without any honor," she rambled over his objections. Her lips were trembling and her hands were shaking so bad that she had to take hold of the corner of his desk to keep them steady. She looked down the length of the desk, and discovered pages from the Coroner's report on the desktop.

"I didn't kill anyone, Yukiko."

"Then he was murdered on your orders."

"You don't really believe that."

"Yes, I do."

"What reason would I have to kill your assistant?" Ryan tired to appeal to the Japanese scientist's rational side. He cleared his throat, straightened his shoulders and sat forward in his chair. The Station's Chief Administrator did not need any more stress, and yet, as he examined the woman's movements more closely, he sensed that there was something terribly wrong with her.

"I am very sorry that he's gone, but I can assure you that I had nothing to do with his death," he continued, gathering the pages of the official autopsy report on Shibata together in his hands. He then gave it to her. "According to this report, Doctor Deckers has determined the cause of Masaki's death as accidental. He could find no evidence of foul play."

Takahashi did not bother to examine the report. She crumpled the papers into a ball in her fist and shook it at him. "This means nothing," she uttered. "You and I both know it is a lie."

"And how would I know that?"

"Because you have no honor."

Ryan rose from his chair. Takahashi wasn't the only one in the room who was out of patience. "I've heard just about enough out of you, Doctor," he shouted. "And I've wasted just about all the time I'm going to with this paranoid delusion of yours. Thank you very much. That will be all!"

"That's not all!" she fired back.

Ryan and Takahashi were now eye to eye. For a moment that seemed like an entire lifetime, they glared at each other. Then she blinked. Trembling, but not with fear or anxiety, she backed away from his desk and turned to leave the office. As she did, her eyes fastened on a picture of Ryan and two handsome young men. She hadn't noticed it before, and only just that morning had he taken it out of the file cabinet and placed it on his desk. The proud father and his sons, she thought, her mind shifting to thoughts of her own son Hiroshi. She took another step and stumbled, catching the toe of her right foot on the heal of her left, like a drunkard struggling to walk a straight line. She could no longer control the tremors in her legs and arms.

Ryan shook his head and sighed. For the last few minutes, he had been trying to figure out what was wrong with the Japanese scientist. He had dismissed the tremors and nervousness as physical manifestations of her high level of anxiety, but could not make sense of her disorientation and paranoia. Then the look of realization came over Ryan's face. Doctor Takahashi was suffering from High Pressure Nervous Syndrome, for all of the telltale signs of the disorder were unmistakable. From all of the reports he had read on his eighteen-month journey from Earth, the report on HPNS had frightened him the most. High Pressure Nervous Syndrome affected nearly one in twenty people, and while it was rarely fatal, most people stricken with the disorder never fully recovered. Their minds simply turned to Jell-O, and they spent the rest of their lives as helpless zombies. Ryan remembered that was one of the reasons why he had instituted a mandatory forty-eight hour rest period for every six hours on the Mining Platform, but she must have overlooked his memorandum.

Takahashi continued her struggle towards the door, then finally surrendered and melted to the floor.

Ryan came out from behind his desk and caught her as she collapsed.

"I think you better take it easy for a few minutes and let me call for a doctor," he said, his bulky American frame looming over the petite Asian woman.

"There's nothing wrong with me," she slurred.

"Doctor, you're suffering with all the classic signs of high pressure nervous syndrome."

"Nonsense. I've been working on the Platform for two years and not been affected once by any of the symptoms."

"Yes, that may be true," Ryan admitted, cradling the woman

in his arms as he knelt on the floor of his office. "But with all of the stress that you've been under in the last few days…"

"I must return to the Platform to complete my report," she stammered.

"The only place you're going is sickbay."

"I no longer recognize your authority."

Ryan placed her gently on the floor, tucking his suit jacket under her head as her body continued to twitch uncontrollably back and forth. "You don't have any choice," he said as he clicked the intercom button on his desk. "Charlie, I need you get Doctor…"

KA-BOOM! All of a sudden, before he could finish another word of his sentence, the Space Station shuddered and shook from an explosion on another deck that did not seem so distant. The shockwave of the blast catapulted him forward, up and over his desk; tumbling, he fell onto the chairs on the other side with a thud. Parts of the recessed ceiling overhead broke loose and came crashing down to the floor. The fluorescent lighting overhead exploded, showering the room with a rain of sparks and plunging them into a Stone Age darkness.

Instinctively, Takahashi curled into a fetal position, shielding her eyes from the raining embers. Ryan clawed his way to her side and placed his body over hers like a protective shield. He felt as if he was in the middle of a World War 2 movie, on board a submarine during an attack, but only one depth charge had hit. He kept waiting for the next explosion that never came.

After a few heartbeats, the intensity of the blast subsided. The power stuttered, then finally, the emergency lights crackled to life.

With a chair to steady him, Ryan struggled to his feet and reached back down for her hand. She saw him, but did not acknowledge him with her eyes. Her body was still trembling from the disorder.

"Are you injured?" he asked, withdrawing his hand.

Takahashi lowered her eyes and did not reply.

Ryan shrugged and turned to his office door.

"Charlie," he shouted through the door, "what the Hell was that?"

Bradford pushed the door open and stood in the entrance, holding his hand to his head. His forehead was bleeding, and from Ryan's point of view, the wound appeared to be a superficial one.

"Explosion on C deck," he replied. "Looks like it took out the whole communications center."

"Are you okay?"

"Yeah. It just looks worse than it is."

"All the same, get it looked at in sickbay," he ordered. Then, as an afterthought, Ryan pointed with a nod towards Takahashi.

"And see that she gets there, too. She's not injured, but I think Doctor Takahashi is suffering from a neurological disorder called High Pressure Nervous Syndrome."

"Okay, boss."

"I'm heading to C deck," he added.

And with that, Ryan was gone.

31

As Ryan raced down the corridor towards C deck, he was both shocked and surprised by what he saw. People and equipment had been knocked to the deck; monitors had been blown out, and fluorescent lighting fixtures dangled in a mishmash of cables from the recessed ceilings above, but the damage hadn't been as severe as he first feared. He watched with pride as his Station personnel, one by one, climbed to their feet, dusted themselves off and began picking up the pieces. Despite assorted cuts and bruises, Ryan saw them pulling together as a team in a moment he would later record as their finest hour.

The Chief Administrator continued running down the hall, then turned the corner into the Communications Center. As he surveyed the room, he saw a jumbled nightmare of broken computers, smashed monitors and sparking cables. The ceiling had completely collapsed, and what was left of the walls had turned charcoal black from the shock wave of the blast. The central imaging chamber, which had been the Station's most important link to Earth and the other colonies, was a molten lump of glass and steel. The Communication Center's only illumination came from the emergency lighting and several small fires that were still burning.

While several maintenance workers were tending the fire with specialized fire-fighting equipment, Cramden and Rudenko were dragging a single body out of the rubble. Ryan went over to lend a hand.

"What's the damage?" he asked.

"Well, we were damn lucky the explosion happened on an inner compartment between decks," Cramden replied. "If it had happened any place else on the Station, we'd all be dead now. As it is, we've lost the subspace transmitter, but we're not completely cut off. We can still send and receive conventional satellite signals as long as we stay in line of sight with Earth or one of the other colonies. The twenty-six minute delay will be a killer, but I'm sure we can manage."

"What about casualties?" Ryan asked Rudenko.

"With the one exception," he responded, indicating the body at hand, "we've been very fortunate. Reports from sickbay indicate that most of the incoming injuries are superficial cuts and abrasions."

"Any idea what happened?" he asked.

"None," Cramden replied, "but it looks like a terrorist attack."

"What makes you think so?"

"When I was stationed on Mars, I saw enough of them to know that this wasn't some equipment malfunction."

Rudenko nodded his head in agreement. "My wife and daughter were killed in an identical attack on Mars years ago when they were using the subspace transmitter to send me a message on Earth," he added, with a choke in his voice.

Ryan looked at his Chief Medical Officer and, for the first time, realized that he was human, like everyone else.

The trio continued dragging the lifeless body out of the Communications Center until they were safely clear of the fire. Once they had reached the outer corridor, Rudenko snapped on a pair of rubber gloves, leaned down on one knee, and turned the body over for a closer look.

"Provenzo," Ryan said in a whisper.

"Do you know this man?" Rudenko asked.

"I met him. Briefly," he replied. "His friends called him Lenny."

"Do you think he was a Martian terrorist?" Cramden inquired.

"No, he was a computer technician," Ryan explained, watching Rudenko examine the body carefully, looking for points of inconsistency. "He must have gotten caught in the explosion."

The Security Chief folded his arms across his chest. "Are you sure about that?"

"No, Cramden, I'm not, but I don't think he was a terrorist. Lenny was so well-liked by everyone, and he just didn't fit the profile of the disgruntled loner who would sacrifice his life for a political cause."

"He wasn't your terrorist," Rudenko interrupted, looking up from the body. "In fact, he's been beaten up pretty badly. Contusions. Multiple lacerations and his shoulder's been pulled right out of joint."

"Are those injuries consistent with the blast?" Ryan asked.

"No, I don't believe so," he replied. "I think this man was beaten unconscious, then left here to die."

"Are you certain?" Cramden asked.

The Chief Medical Officer pointed at Lenny's face. "Look at his mouth," Rudenko stated. "He's been kicked in the jaw. Probably fractured. There's even a partial shoe print."

"Good Christ," Ryan gasped.

"I want to get a photo of that," Cramden said. "We might be able to find the shoe that matches it later."

"Poor bastard," Ryan muttered. Even though he had spent less than five minutes with Provenzo, he knew that Rachel had grown very fond of Lenny, and Ryan had wasted more than one or two jealous thoughts over his rival. He realized just how silly he had been, but he still couldn't help struggling with ambivalent feelings about the dead computer technician. Finally, he pulled himself together.

"Cramden, I want you to seal this entire section off, then I want you and your people to go through the Center with a fine tooth comb," he ordered. "I want you to find the sonuvabitch who did this to Provenzo, no matter what it takes, and when you find him, I want ten minutes alone with him."

"Yes, sir."

Rudenko said, "I'll make sure the body gets to the Coroner's office."

"No! I don't want Deckers involved," Ryan returned. "I want you to conduct the autopsy yourself."

"Me?"

"The fewer people who know about this, the better. In fact, I don't want either of you talking to anyone about this, or even using the word 'terrorist'. There's no reason to cause a panic throughout the Station," he said, lowering his voice to a whisper. "Until I say otherwise, we're calling this an accident caused by equipment malfunction. Do I make myself clear?"

"Yes, sir," they both replied.

"Let's get cracking," he concluded. "There's a killer loose on this Station and it's up to us to find him."

Ryan nodded at Cramden and Rudenko, then turned back in the direction of his office. He walked past the devastation of the Communication Center at a fast clip, his head down as if lost in thought.

A heartbeat later, one of the shadows in the darkened corridor lengthened into the figure of a man who followed Ryan around a corner.

Suddenly, the Chief Administrator was no longer there. Shadow Man turned to the left, then turned to the right, looking for him. Ryan leaped out, grabbed the Shadow Man from behind and shoved him against the wall.

"Okay, pal, enough with the hide and go seek," he exclaimed, holding the mystery man's head against the bulkhead. "You better start telling me who you are and why you've been following me...and you'd better do it fast."

"It's not what you think, Mister Ryan."

"Explain it to me then."

32

With a certain degree of apprehension, Reinhardt approached the door to his Presidential Suite after several knocks and glanced through the privacy hole. At first, he had suspected the knocks belonged to Ryan; then he remembered that, after their last encounter, his old protégé would have simply barged through the door, without knocking. Next, he thought the knocks belonged to one of the men in dark suits that Susan Ryan had assigned to 'look after him', but he dismissed that

thought with a shrug. The large, knuckle-dragging Neander-
thals had never learned the fine point of subtlety, and would
have banged on the door with their brutish foreheads. Finally,
after reducing all of the possibilities to a single individual, he
looked to the other side of the door and was not too surprised to
see that it was Rachel Westin.

"What are you doing here?" he demanded, pulling Rachel
out of the corridor and slamming the door behind her.

"Don't worry, Edward," she reassured him. "No one saw
me."

"I thought I told you never to contact me."

She stared at the floor, unable to make eye contact. "I need
my travel documents and I want out of our deal."

"What's the problem, Rachel?"

"I just want out."

"Impossible."

She walked into the sitting room of his suite. It wasn't the
first time that she had been there, but she was determined that it
would be her last. She stopped in the middle of the room and
threw up her arms in distress.

"You know, this isn't at all how you described it," she cried.
"No one was supposed to die."

The portly figure of Reinhardt approached Rachel from behind and placed both of his hands on her shoulders. Tenderly,
he started massaging her tense muscles in an attempt to relieve
her anxiety, like a father taking the pains of the world away
from his only daughter.

"I'm sorry that you are in such pain, my dear," he said softly,
almost a whisper, "but you mustn't blame yourself for what's
happened. Shibata died of natural causes, according to the
coroner's report. And Lenny…poor, sweet, dear Lenny…he was
just in the wrong place at the wrong time."

She craned her neck around and looked into his eyes for
the first time, while he continued to ply her shoulders with lov-

ing affection. "Edward, I know that. I just don't like this whole setup, and I don't like having to lie to him."

"Trust me, Rachel. Ryan doesn't know you're lying to him, and what he doesn't know won't hurt him."

"But he deserves better than that."

"And where was this pious understanding of right and wrong all those years while you were sleeping with a married man," Reinhardt asked, "or did you just suddenly grow a conscience while you've been here?"

Rachel hung her head. "I just can't do it any more."

"Look, we made a deal," he reminded her, his voice deepening. "You're not going to get your letters of transit or the money I promised you until after I am satisfied the job is done. Besides, you wouldn't want me talking with Ryan about your duplicity in all of this, would you?"

"Are you threatening me again, Edward?"

"No, my dear, I am merely reminding you of your obligation to me."

"And suppose I just go to Ryan myself with what I already know."

Reinhardt's paternal caresses turned suddenly violent as his hands wrapped about her delicate neck and he began to squeeze her throat. She fought to break free, but that made him tighten his grip even more.

"Don't threaten me," he growled. "Don't ever threaten me."

She nodded, fearful that she would be choked to death if she didn't agree with him.

"You've got a job to do," he added, "and I expect you to do it. Period!"

She nodded again.

After a long, breathless moment, he released his grasp and she tumbled to the floor, coughing, choking and trying to catch her breath. He looked down at her with a blank expression on his face, for the old man could summon neither pity nor sympathy for the blonde beauty. Instead he wiped the palms of his hands together, as if cleansing himself of her, and walked over to the entrance of his suite.

"Now get out," he ordered, opening the door.

Rachel scrambled to her feet and raced out of the Presidential Suite. The look on her face revealed that she was literally frightened to death, but Reinhardt did not seem to care. He simply slammed the door behind her. The old man then picked up his personal comlink and keyed in a numerical sequence.

"I've got another little problem…" he said into the device.

33

Ryan released Shadow Man from his grasp, took a step or two away, then turned back around to face him.

"So why all the cloak and dagger?" he asked. "Why didn't you just come right out and tell me you were my personal body-guard?"

Shadow Man straightened up. "When Mister Bradford first hired me to protect you, he insisted that I keep a really low profile."

"Low profile? Well, you certainly achieved that objective. I thought I was going crazy every time I saw a shadow move."

"You weren't supposed to see me at all."

Ryan paced back and forth, stroking his chin. For a moment, he was lost in deep thought, then he asked, "But why? I've never been in any danger here. All my enemies are back on Earth."

"Really? Would you like me to provide you with a list, starting with the terrorist factions on Mars, or the environmental crazies from Earth, or Edward Reinhardt? You may not realize it, Mister Ryan, but when you accepted this post, you became the most powerful man in the Solar System...and the most hated."

Ryan stopped pacing and looked at Shadow Man for another moment. What he saw frightened him, but he didn't draw away.

"I think I understand."

"With the raw materials of this planet at your fingertips, you control the fate of entire nations; the whole System, for that matter," Shadow Man added. "You could tip the very balance of power, if you sided with the rebels on Mars; or crush a nation, if it failed to yield to your authority. At this moment, you are the ultimate power in the universe, and I feel humbled to serve you."

"Yes, yes, I see."

"Just say the word, master, and I will do anything for you," he concluded, falling to one knee and bowing his head.

Ryan hesitated, then said, "You're fired."

"Mister Ryan?"

"I don't need followers or disciplines," he explained, pulling the man to his feet, "and I don't want to be worshipped like some kind of tin god. I agreed to take this job because I thought I could do some good for the people of the Earth, not to be proclaimed as some sort of messiah or feared as some kind of dictator. When I left my family and friends back in Baltimore, I had only one purpose in mind, and that was to serve my country and the world. Not to lead."

"But don't you see, Mister Ryan? You can also serve humanity by taking on the mantle of leadership and putting an end to tyranny and oppression once and for all time. You could use this power for good."

"End tyranny and oppression by becoming a tyrant?" Ryan mused, then shook his head. "If there's one lesson that I learned as a politician, it's the inevitability of the old adage that power corrupts, and absolute power corrupts absolutely. I've watched far too many good, decent men, who were elected to Congress, become drunk with power once they reached the Hill..."

Shadow Man listened.

"...and I must confess that I drank from that well, myself, more than once," he continued. "That's the problem with power. Once you get a taste for it, you become addicted, and then you find yourself doing things that you would have never done before just to stay refreshed. The first time, you tell yourself you'll only do it once; the next time, you're convinced that it's for the common good, and then, before long, you're compromising every principle you ever hard."

"I think I understand."

"Good!" Ryan exclaimed, patting him on the back. "Now go back to Charlie Bradford and tell him he'll be looking for another job if I find another one of you spooks dogging me. I can take care of myself."

Shadow Man nodded as Ryan walked away, leaving him standing in the shadows of the corridor.

34

Rachel felt a rush of adrenaline as she slipped out of the shadows and made a quick scan of the Communications Center. The dark room, which was only illuminated by light shining through the doors from the outer corridor, looked like a tornado had touched down, and whirled all of its extensive communications equipment into a twisted rubble of metal, wire, and plastic. She had managed to slip past the Security Guards during their routine shift change, and now found herself scanning the room for something she could use against Reinhardt. She hadn't believed a word he told her, and was desperate to find the one piece of evidence that would tie him to the murder of Lenny Provenzo.

Rachel had spent the last five years of her life under Reinhardt's thumb, and now, more than anything, was anxious to be rid of him. She had made one stupid mistake in judgment and found herself paying for that mistake every day of her life since. When she had been hired by a major industrial concern to conduct a routine safety study of the radiation levels seeping through the domes on Phobos, Reinhardt offered to pay her several hundred thousand dollars to manipulate the results of her findings. At first, she didn't want his money; but then, when he threatened to go public with the news of her illicit relationship with Ryan, Rachel reconsidered. In the report, she concluded the faulty domes were not responsible for the instances of genetic mutation, and saved the manufacturer millions of dollars in lawsuits. She thought that would be the end of things, but Reinhardt had other plans. Instead of paying the money he had promised, he used the bogus results of Rachel's study to blackmail her further.

Rachel didn't have any illusions about herself; she knew what kind of woman she was. She realized that she cut corners and often circumvented established protocol for the sake of expediency. How else could she prove that she was more than just a beautiful woman? Men like Ryan and Reinhardt had never fully accepted her as a serious scientist, so she had to work twice as hard as other women just to demonstrate her true worth. And if that meant taking a bribe to falsify some report or spying on the man she loved, then that's what she was prepared to do. She was not above blackmail herself, especially if it meant she could be rid of Reinhardt once and for all.

Stepping carefully over the shards of glass and steel, she waded through the broken monitors and smashed equipment.

Then she rifled through several overturned file drawers and saw nothing of interest. After she closed the last drawer, she looked around for the data port. She was about to hack into the Station's mainframe database when she heard footsteps approaching. She ducked quickly down behind the unit just as the door opened — but not quickly enough.

"Alright, come out of there," the Security Guard ordered, placing his right hand on top of his weapon and shining his flashlight in her face.

Reluctantly, she climbed to her feet and came out from behind the rubble.

"Who are you? What are you doing here? This area is off limits to all civilians and Station personnel."

"My name is Doctor Westin," she said, trying to shield her eyes from his bright light. "I'm the Chief Science Officer."

The Security Guard punched her name into his data pad. "Oh, yes, Doctor *Rachel* Westin. Female. Caucasian. Age 35. Ph.D. in Astrophysics," he said, reading the information from his miniature screen. "According to this, your last assignment was on the Martian colonies and you transferred here last month. Don't you know this is a restricted area? What were you doing here?"

"I just came to send a quick message…"

"All outgoing communications are now being routed through the command center," he reported, somewhat coldly. He stepped closer and held her chin in his hand, turning her face from side to side. Her eyes were red and puffy, and her black mascara had run down her face and formed two big blotches that made her look like a raccoon. He looked at the woman's neck more closely, and noticed two red handprints where Reinhardt had tried to strangle her. "I think you'd better start telling me the truth, Doctor."

"Please. I didn't know this was a restricted area," she said, trying to turn away. "You don't understand…it's not what you think…" Rachel's mind started rotating through all the possible scenarios, and settled on one quickly. "My boyfriend and I just had a fight . . . and . . . I came here to send a message home . . . "

"Perhaps, I should escort you back to your quarters?" the security guard said, walking her to the door. "We wouldn't want this 'boyfriend' of yours to give you anymore trouble tonight, would we."

Rachel swallowed hard. "No, that won't be necessary. I know my way."

"I insist…"

She stuck with the Security Guard until they passed the recreation hall, then cleverly mingled with familiar faces in the crowd to lose him. She moved quickly through the Station personnel and hoped that he wouldn't follow her. She went around the corner and paused in the shadows. She peered back from her cover and saw him looking about, perplexed. He probably wasn't used to someone giving him the slip so easily. Then again, she wasn't just anyone.

Quickly, she circled back to the Communications Center and tucked herself into the shadows. She could see the Security Guards stationed at each of the doors, including the one that she had just left. They made routine checks on their respective access points every ten minutes, and she noticed that when they made their rounds they neglected the fire exit as a possible means of unauthorized entry. The Security Guards must have thought the exit was still alarmed. But she reasoned the alarm had been deactivated during the fire and never turned back on. As the Security Guards patrolled the access points on each side of the room, she slipped in through the fire exit.

Once inside, she moved quickly to the mainframe. She flipped a switch on the data port and the panel slid open, revealing a computer monitor and code key. A keyboard slid out and she punched in a few codes. She went to a search program, then punched in "Lenny Provenzo" and "Jovian lifeform." She was hoping Lenny's three-dimensional scanning program had not only recorded his research data but also some clue as to the identity of his killer. While the message 'SEARCHING' appeared on the screen, she looked around the room at the damage.

She spotted Lenny's baseball cap, partially buried and obscured by the rubble, and it brought tears back to her eyes. As she reached down to pick it up, she shook out all of the debris that had collected in the crown. Lenny Provenzo may have been the one man who truly loved her and she never gave him a chance.

The search ended with no matches. Rachel frowned. Whatever new information Lenny had discovered about the Jovians, he took it with him. Along with the identity of his killer.

She shut down the computer and closed the compartment, then slipped back out, tucking Lenny's cap into the waist of her pantsuit. When she didn't see any of the Security Guards, she vanished back into the shadows and disappeared.

35

In the forward observation chamber of the Mining Platform, Takahashi was feeling desperate as she searched the clouds for some sign of the Jovian lifeforms. She sat with her face against the Plexiglas of the observation window and her hands cupped around the corners of her eyes. She scanned from the left to the right, then back again. She knew that if she failed to make contact with them, she had brought dishonor down upon herself. The diminutive Japanese scientist glanced over her shoulder at the chronometer in the rear of the compartment and realized she was quickly running out of time. She knew the mining operation would begin as planned on Monday, and feared what that might mean to the Jovians. It might as well have been a million years for there was no sign of them.

She was still suffering with uncontrollable tremors, her hands and body shaking so badly that she had draw herself up into a fetus, her knees steadying the head on her shoulders. In all of the confusion in sickbay, she had managed to give Bradford the slip and had stolen a shuttle without authorization. She knew that probably meant her career, but she had run out of options.

For an instant, Doctor Yukiko Takahashi closed her eyes in an effort to settle her thoughts. She had often daydreamed of studying life on other planets while she was an undergraduate at New Haven, and her assignment to Jupiter was the answer to many years of wishful thinking. She felt more comfortable in orbit around the gas giant than any other place on Earth, even New Tokyo, where she had been born and raised in a very traditional household; and the United States, where she had been educated and met her husband Hiroki. Like most Japanese who studied abroad, she had been rejected by her own people, and made the object of suspicion by others. Even her own parents, who still bore thirty-year-old scars from the great trade wars, clung to many isolationist beliefs. They disapproved of her choice of schools and refused to acknowledge her doctorate when she had completed her studies. Her decision to marry an astronaut, and live on one of the off-world colonies, was made more of necessity than choice. Only Masaki and her late husband had known the reason why she left Earth, and now both of them were dead. Perhaps that was the reason why the Jovians meant so much to her. Like her son, they still had a chance for a full life, without fear or apprehension. Each time they drew near the Platform, they brought what she perceived was a wide-eyed innocence. And just like her own child, she felt they needed her as protector and guardian.

Feeling a sudden sensation in the back of her head, Takahashi opened her eyes to discover the room was spinning all around her. She struggled to pull her body upright, but became instantly aware that she was fighting a loosing battle. She felt like someone who had had too much to drink and could no longer control herself. In one final, last ditch effort, she clawed at the Plexiglas window to stand, but instead slumped to the floor, a mass of shakes and quivers.

36

Ryan opened the door to his quarters and discovered Rachel standing in the entrance. At first, he was surprised to see her, then he recognized just how upset she was. Her eyes were red and puffy, and her black mascara had run all over her face. She held back her tears as Ryan took her right hand and pulled her into the middle of his room.

"Rachel," he asked softly, "are you okay?"

"No," she replied, "I don't think I'll ever be okay again."

"I'm sorry. I should have told you the news myself. Lenny's death must have come as quite a shock to you," Ryan said, somewhat bewildered. "Maybe, if I had, I could have saved you a lot of trouble. Just what did you hope to accomplish by going down to the Communications Center…?"

He broke off as she gasped and started to crumple. She went to her knees before he could catch her, clutching Lenny's baseball cap to her heart. He immediately recognized it, and all of his questions became suddenly academic. Moments before she arrived at his quarters, he had received a call from one of Cramden's Security Guards who had caught her snooping in the restricted area. He had suspected her of being the Martian terrorist. But Ryan knew better.

She looked up at him, struggling to control herself. "People weren't supposed to die. Not people you know," she finally said.

"I know."

"I just keep thinking that there was something I could have done."

"No, there was nothing either of us could have done."

Rachel felt sad, depressed, angry, agitated, confused—a hundred different emotions all at once. She fought to control herself, but could no longer hold back the flood of tears and started crying her eyes out.

Ryan didn't know how to respond, and without much thought, reached for the box of tissues on his nightstand.

"You don't understand," she replied, sobbing as she took a tissue from him. "I feel responsible for what happened to Lenny."

"Nonsense. There wasn't anything you could have done," he tried to reassure her.

"No...you just don't understand."

"I'm sorry."

"Oh, Mitchell!" she cried and burst into tears once more. "Hold me. Please . . . just hold me."

Ryan gathered Rachel tightly in a protective embrace and just held her.

Saturday

37

In the virtual reality center, Reinhardt was playing a round of golf in an effort to fight off a case of mental fatigue. The portly, seventy-year old man had been pushing himself to the limits of his endurance, and while he was satisfied with the results of his labor, he was also very, very tired. Other men his age might have settled for a long afternoon respite, but personally he loathed naps, associating them with sleep and death. He knew there would be plenty of time to sleep when he was finally laid to rest in a pine box, and preferred to seize every moment he had left, eyes wide open. Golf was the only thing that relaxed him.

Alone, except for a virtual golf caddie, Reinhardt walked onto the fourth tee and teed up the Penfold Hearts—his ball of choice which he had programmed into the computer simulation. Off to the side, he took one or two careful, concentrated, practice swings. Then he took up his stance, addressing the ball straight on, and brought the head of his golf club back in a wide slow arc. With his eyes glued to the ball, he snapped his wrists and whipped the club head through. The ball soared about two hundred feet, paused elegantly in the air, then dropped down onto the fairway.

"Excellent shot," his virtual caddie commented, flat and lifeless.

Reinhardt nodded his head. "Yes, it was."

He started walking towards the ball, feeling better already. Throughout the long years, he had found few physical activities as stimulating and conversely relaxing as a good round of golf. Back in the old days, when he had been a freshman in Congress and found himself overwhelmed with trivial committee work, he would sneak out to a favorite course just over the Potomac River in Virginia. Nothing quite relieved the stress of his political duties like the peaceful tranquillity of that eighteen-hole course in Arlington. Today, he was shooting a smaller but more challenging course at Diamond Ridge in the suburbs of Baltimore; earlier in the week, he had played the Royal Saint Marks just outside London.

Of course, he knew that he wasn't really in Baltimore, and hadn't recently traveled to Great Britain, but the computer simulation made it appear virtually real to him. While the room was only slightly bigger than his suite, projections on the four walls, ceiling and floor provided the illusion of a golf course that seemed to stretch out for miles in every direction. There was actually no fairway, no green, no tee and no Penfold Hearts—only the golf club that he was holding was real. The holographic images projected by the computer, which were not unlike those projected in the central imaging chamber, fooled his mind into thinking that he was on a golf course, shooting a tremendous game. If he had wanted to serve an ace at Wimbledon or hit a home run out of the park at old Wrigley Field or score the winning run at the Superbowl, all he had to do was program the simulation and the computer took care of everything else. But he preferred swinging at golf balls.

"I thought I might find you here," Ryan said, walking slowly but deliberately into the computer simulation.

"Golf is the sport of kings, Mitch. You should know that," Reinhardt said, passing his club to the golf caddie. "Golf originated in Scotland in the fifteenth century, and was the game that separated the aristocracy from the rest of the rabble."

"Really," he replied, dully.

Ryan reached for a nine iron from Reinhardt's set of American Ben Hogan's and approached him with the club held up in the air. For an instant, the old man didn't know whether Ryan was going to break it over his head, or use it to hit his Penfold hearts golf ball. He did not move an inch, but beads of perspiration formed on his forehead. Ryan continued his approach. He addressed the ball, swung quickly, lifting his head, and shanked the Penfold Hearts almost at a right angle. A foot of virtual turf flew up, but the ball bounced onto the course.

"You're slicing to the right again," Reinhardt shouted. "You never could make that shot with a nine iron."

Ryan watched the ball trail off down the course and groaned. "Since when did you become such an expert?"

"I taught you everything you know," he said, selecting an iron from his golf bag and taking one or two careless practice swings.

"I guess that's the real reason why you have so little left," Ryan replied. He slipped the nine iron back into the bag and pulled a stitched leather cover over the club's wooden head.

"I could beat you on my worst day."

"You've not beaten once me in over twenty years."

"We've not played in twenty years," Reinhardt returned. "Not since you made such an ass of yourself at the Hampton Invitational."

"Jordan Baker was cheating!"

"So what!" the older man exclaimed. "Everybody cheats at something—cards, taxes, tests, relationships. It's a fact of life.

Miss Baker was just unlucky enough to get caught at it by you." He stared at Ryan with a soulless gaze. "Didn't you learn anything from me?"

"Too much," he quipped. "Particularly about cheating."

"Why must you always reduce everything down to its simplest terms? Black or white, good or evil. Haven't you learned yet that there's more gray in the Solar System than any other color?" Reinhardt asked rhetorically.

"Is that so?"

"Take this golf simulation, for example," he continued to press his point. "It isn't real. It's just some elaborate computer program designed to cheat your mind and senses."

Reinhardt continued to practice his golf swing, only partially aware of his place in the conversation. Annoyed, Ryan stormed over to the emergency override switch and smashed it, breaking the safety mechanism with a single blow of his fist. Instantly, the eighteen-hole illusion was gone and all that was left were four blank walls. Reinhardt chose not to react. Instead, he brought the head of his golf club back in a wide, slow arc and followed through with a stroke.

"No, it isn't," Ryan said. "This is a computer simulation, nothing more. What men, like you and me, do with it is what makes the program good or evil."

"Come, come now, Mitch. You mustn't be so bitter. I only had your best interests at heart."

Ryan relaxed his fist. The cutting edge was red and swollen, and he knew that it would soon show a bruise. "I suppose this is the part when you tell me how much like a son I've been to you."

Reinhardt started to reply, but was cut off before he could say a word.

"I guess you had my best interests at heart all along, Edward," he added with a grimace. "You wetted my thirst for power, convincing me that it was in the best interest of my constituency, and then, when I was most vulnerable, you plied me with all of those expensive gifts. The committee appoints. The tax variances. The female interns. You gave me everything to keep me thirsty, but never anything to quench my thirst. All because you had me convinced that it was in my best interest. Did it ever occur to you that I might grow to resent you for all of that?"

"Well, no, but I can see how that was a mistake."

"A very big mistake. But that's all in the past now. I don't want any more of your gifts or special favors, and I certainly don't want anything more to do with you. I'm my own man now."

Reinhardt grinned. "You can't just cut me out."

"Watch me."

"You can't just run away."

"Can't I?" Ryan smiled confidently. "I'm not running away. I'm right here and I plan to stay right here. I'm just not your man anymore."

"But we're family…"

"Well," Ryan interrupted, "you may be a member of my political lobby in Washington and the grandfather of my two boys, but you are nothing to me." He seized the club out of the other man's arthritic hands and shoved it into his golf bag. Then he turned to leave. "When I divorced your daughter Susan, I divorced you and all of those suits you work for."

"Divorces end marriages, Mitch, not partnerships. The two of us are joined for life."

"We are nothing. Get that!" Ryan held up his swollen hand with its thumb and forefinger locked into a circle, and thrust it into his face. "Zero. Zilch…nothing!"

Reinhardt staggered back, surprised. "How ironic," he mumbled under his breath. "I had a very special gift I was going to give you."

"Didn't you just hear me? I don't want anything from you."

"Well, then, let's just call it a peace offering."

Ryan started walking towards the exit. When he reached it, he paused with his back to the other man, listening.

"That liability we spoke of?" Reinhardt said. "I took care of it myself."

"Just like you took care of Shibata," he sighed. "Why, Edward? Provenzo was no threat to you. He was a tech head, and wouldn't have harmed a fly."

"I had nothing to do with his death," the old man replied, shaking his head. "I understand terrorist factions are being blamed for that one. Perhaps you should take it up with them."

Ryan hesitated. "I'm beginning to think the revolution on Mars is just another lie. I'm beginning to think that you and those others like you orchestrated the whole thing just to keep Earth and the colonies in line. To make them think you had their best interests in mind when in fact you just needed an excuse to seize power."

"You give me too much credit. I'm just a concerned citizen who wants the best for everyone."

"Spare me your poetic notions about civic pride and just tell me what you've done this time," Ryan demanded, turning to him with a glare.

Reinhardt acquiesced with a slight nod of his head. "Takahashi will no longer be a liability."

Ryan's jaw dropped. He stared at his former benefactor for a moment, appalled. Then he growled, "For your sake, she better be alive and breathing. Now, what did you do to her?"

"Nothing much. I just helped her fall asleep."

"Where?"

"The Platform."

"Damn!" Ryan swore, opening his comlink with the flick of a wrist, then typed the access number into the keyboard. He had warned her not to go near there, and yet she must have disobeyed his order.

"Don't bother," the old man retorted. "I already took the precaution of disabling the communications link to the Mining Platform."

"You sonuvabitch, what else aren't you telling me?"

"Nothing…"

Ryan typed another sequence into the keypad.

"Charlie," he shouted into the comlink, "have a team of medics waiting for me in the docking bay! Priority alpha emergency!"

Reinhardt took a step toward the door, but Ryan caught a glimpse of him out of the corner of his eye. He grabbed the seventy-year-old man by the lapels of his designer jacket, spun him around and flung him to the center of the room. Reinhardt hit the floor with a thud.

"You're not going anywhere," Ryan shouted, his voice exploding off the four walls in a sonic boom. "You're going to wait right here until I get back. And you had better start praying that she's alive and well, because if she isn't, you're going to wish to Christ that you had never been born!"

He yanked the comlink out of the central console and tossed it out of the exit. Then he flipped a switch on the computer simulation panel and smashed the main relay with his fist. The room was suddenly transformed into a treacherous mountain range on the rust-colored surface of Mars. Reinhardt lunged for the edge of a nearby cliff, grabbed hold and hung on for dear life.

"No, Mitchell! You know that I can't stand heights!"

"With the manual override broken and the main relay smashed, the best that you can do is to hang on until I get back," he said, turning to the exit door, "or you could always try climbing down."

"No!" he pleaded.

"But you'd better watch your step," he added. "The drop off is fifteen thousand feet straight down."

Ryan locked and sealed the door.

38

Thirty minutes later, Ryan, Rudenko, a Medical Technician and a Pilot were scrambling through the Platform, past the empty bunks in the aft compartment, through the central office complex and into the connecting corridor. They paused only long enough for Ryan to flood the room with a new air mixture, then continued through the heavy airlock door and into the forward observation chamber. He half expected to find Takahashi sprawled out on the deck with one hand around her throat and the other grasping for the comlink. That was the way they had found Shibata. But when they finally reached her, she was resting peacefully, like a sleeping princess in a fairy tale.

"Nitrogen asphyxia," Rudenko said to his assistant, bending down on one knee and pressing two fingers against the side of her neck.

"She probably never knew what hit her," the Medical Technician replied, turning to Ryan and the Pilot. "The overpowering mixture of nitrogen gas just sort of crept up and carried her away."

"Hey, I've got a pulse," Rudenko exclaimed. "Get me 100cc's of adrenaline."

At once, the two men sprang into action. While his assistant filled a syringe from a bottle of adrenaline, Rudenko straddled the woman's upper torso, pumping her chest with his hands. He locked his lips over hers and started mouth-to-mouth resuscitation, using the same rhythm he had been pumping her chest. He continued breathing into her lungs for a few minutes, then climbed back on top of her body and resumed pumping her chest.

The Medical Technician instantly followed his lead. Once he had finished injecting her with the stimulant, he pulled a small, lightweight respirator from his equipment pack. Then he placed its black rubber mask over her mouth and renewed attempts to restart her breathing by pumping a squeeze bag.

Takahashi did not respond to their actions.

Ryan knelt beside her, at the woman's head, and gently stroked her short, black hair. As difficult as it was confronting her with his skepticism regarding the Jovian lifeforms, he had no real quarrel with Doctor Takahashi. In fact, he realized now that he liked and respected the Japanese scientist and believed her to be genuine, which was more than he could say for Reinhardt or the others. In her face, Ryan saw the person that he used to be before he succumbed to all of the temptations of power. He saw a person of tremendous integrity and humility whose unswerving devotion to her principles despite overwhelming adversity was more important than life itself. And even though he disagreed with her theories, he admired her for her integrity. He just hoped they could bring her back.

"Come on, breathe!" the Medical Technician cried out, plying her with fresh air.

Takahashi remained still.

"She's not responding. We're gonna lose her. Come on, damnit!" Rudenko swore at her, pounding on the woman's delicate chest.

"You're killing her!" Ryan shouted beside him, feeling the urge to do something…anything.

The Pilot held him back. "No, they know what they're doing," she said. "Just let them work."

Rudenko continued to pound on her chest.

"Breathe, damnit! Breathe!"

"Come on, breathe!" his assistant repeated.

Ryan stared down into Takahashi's face; her porcelain features had gone ashen. Panicked, he looked from Rudenko to the Medical Technician and cried, "Help her, goddamnit!"

Frantically, the Chief Medical Officer and his assistant struggled to keep her alive as her features grew more and more pale.

"Fight, goddamnit..." Rudenko shouted, pumping hard and fast on her chest with the palms of his hands.

"FIGHT!" his assistant completed.

Ryan reached out to the Japanese scientist and gently squeezed her hand. "You can't just die on me like this," he whispered in her ear. "The fate of the Jovians rests in your hands. They're counting on you to make their voices heard." He thought about his words for a moment, then added, "But they're not the only ones. I'm relying on your judgment to keep me honest."

Takahashi's eyelids fluttered.

"Yukiko!" he cried, squeezing her hand tightly.

Rudenko continued to massage her heart and force air into her lungs through cardiopulmonary resuscitation. In a matter of moments, or perhaps mere heartbeats, her face twitched and her hands clenched and unclenched in spasm. The color was returning to the ice-cold features of her face.

"Come on...you can do it..." Rudenko urged.

"Come on...you can do it..." the Medical Technician repeated.

Ryan added, "Yukiko...you can do it. Don't quit on me now."

Finally, with a feeble cough, Takahashi pushed the mask away from her mouth and started to breathe on her own. She choked at first, struggling for each breath. But then, gradually, the Asian woman began to breathe and exhale the fresh air in her lungs, with some difficulty.

"All right!" the Medical Technician exclaimed.

"Thank God," Rudenko prayed. "I thought we'd lost her."

Ryan and the others couldn't believe their eyes, but the proof was right before them. It seemed impossible that she was still alive, but the Chief Administrator was beginning to believe that anything was possible.

With a tremendous weight lifted from his shoulders, Doctor Rudenko climbed to his feet and sighed a deep sigh of relief. His face was beet red and he was sweating from every pore in his body. The Medical Technician rocked back on his haunches, relieved, and tossed his boss a towel. Rudenko used it to wipe the perspiration from his face. The Pilot was crying tears of joy.

"*Domo arigato*," she said to Ryan, with a slight nod of her head.

"*Dozo, nami-mo*," he replied modestly.

"C'mon," Rudenko ordered, still out of breath. "We've got to get her back to sickbay and put her in a hyperbaric chamber."

"Right," his assistant replied.

Ryan was concerned. "Will she be okay, doc?"

Rudenko looked down at Takahashi for a moment or two, then pulled Ryan to the side.

"She's experienced a very severe trauma to the lungs. Unless I can get normal pressure restored, she may be forced to use a respirator for the rest of her life. The next few hours will be critical."

"But will she be okay?" Ryan asked.

"I think so," Rudenko replied, patting him on the shoulder.

"Thank God," he sighed.

"The question is will you be okay, if I leave you on your own?"

Ryan raised an eyebrow in confusion, then the look of realization settled upon his face. The *Montgolfier* was designed as a four-man craft and might prove dangerous with five.

"I don't think we can all fit back safely in the airship," Rudenko stated the obvious, "and I really do need my assistant at hand just in case something goes wrong…"

"…and that leaves me the odd man out," Ryan concluded.

"Sorry."

Ryan took a deep breath and smiled at his Doctor. Then he looked down at Takahashi and exhaled with a sigh.

"Okay," he said, "Guess I'll just catch the next one going my way."

39

A few minutes later, Rudenko and his Medical Technician were wheeling Takahashi on a gurney toward the docking hatch. Ryan walked alongside, holding her hand in his. She was still feeling lightheaded, and could barely breathe without choking, but she was starting to come around. Probably, after a few days in a decompression chamber, followed by two or three weeks of rest in sickbay, she would be able to return to her duties.

"You're going to be okay. There's nothing to worry about," he reassured her. "The doc's just taking you to sickbay for some routine tests."

"Mister Ryan," she said weakly, "you are not a very good liar."

"No, I suppose I'm not," he confessed. "I've spent a lifetime learning how to lie, but I guess my heart was never really in it."

"I have spent a lifetime studying other forms of life," she confessed, "but I never had the courage to look at my own life and consider the humanity of others around me."

"We picked good jobs, didn't we?"

Takahashi smiled, and in turn, so did Ryan.

When they reached the air lock, Ryan helped them carry her halfway up the ladder, then weightlessness did all of the rest. In a matter of moments, they had secured her to a seat and strapped themselves in.

"Take good care of her, doc," Ryan said, shaking Rudenko's hand.

"You know I will."

"See you in a couple of hours."

"She should be stable by then," Rudenko assured him.

Ryan shut the hatch above his head and spun the wheel lock closed. The bank of lights flashed momentarily from red to yellow. He climbed back down the ladder, and felt the weight of gravity pulling on his lower torso as he stepped down on the metal deck. His actions seemed routine, like he had been doing them all his life, and yet, upon reflection, he remembered his first time down, just six days earlier. A lot had happened in six days.

He paused at the bottom of the ladder, listening for the sound of the docking ring to release its hold on the *Montgolfier*, and breathed a sigh of relief as the metal clamps clanked open and sent the airship speeding on its way back to the Station. At last satisfied, he strolled back to the forward compartment.

When he reached the forward observation chamber, he looked out of the large circular window. At first, the view startled him, much like his first look at the Great Red Eye of Jupiter from inside the miniscule airship. Instinctively, he grabbed for the nearest object to him and held on for dear life. But in time, he became accustomed to the view, and took tentative steps away from his lifeline, only to go racing back the moment he lost his nerve. Finally, after what seemed to be an eternity, he bravely approached the concave window, cautious but unafraid.

The view from the observation window was spectacular. He looked right down into the vast ocean of dense gas and floating clouds of the Jovian atmosphere, which was the very soul of the gas giant Jupiter.

He pressed his face against the Plexiglas and cupped his hands around the corners of his eyes, so he could focus his attention forward. He looked from side to side, but he could see no sign of the Jovian lifeforms. Ryan was annoyed, but also, at the same time, awestruck.

He backed away from the window and flicked open his comlink.

"Charlie, this is Ryan," he spoke into the link, glancing up at the Station. "I want you to set up a meeting with the delegates from the United Planets..."

From his vantage point, the Space Station looked like a Christmas tree floating in the upper cloud stratum of Jupiter, its thousand pin-points of light twinkling like Yuletide ornaments against the darkness of space. At nearly three-hundred yards in diameter, the massive structure was largest object in the night sky, and yet it was still dwarfed by the billowing sea of clouds that swirled up from the surface to embrace it. He marveled at the incredible feat of engineering that had built the Station and put it into orbit, but also realized that it was so vulnerable. For the moment, however, the Space Station seemed tranquil and at peace, all alone in the night.

Suddenly, there was a blinding flash near the reactor core, and the lights on the Station's towering spires flickered off, then on, and finally off. Ryan thought the flash itself looked like a super nova in the darkness, and as the circle of light radiated outward, the leading edge was blue-white. Reds and oranges mixed with yellows at the center of the blast as the ball of fire gained intensity. From where he was standing, the scene had an eerie sense of unreality about it.

The leading edge of the shock wave radiated outward in all directions, like the blast wave of a nuclear explosion. He saw that the shock wave was going to hit the Mining Platform, but there was nothing he could do.

"Oh, my God!"

Just then, the entire Platform shuddered with the impact, and he was catapulted across the forward compartment. The shock wave was accompanied by an incredible blast of light that flooded the forward observation chamber with blinding shafts of blue and white. Ryan put his hands over his head and buried his eyes. The impact of the blast threw the Mining Platform forward, and as the shock wave passed, pushed it backward in its wake.

Overhead, the fluorescent lights that were recessed in the ceiling exploded into a shower of sparks, and several sections of the lighting conduit broke loose and came crashing to the floor. Without a moment's hesitation, he rolled under a desk and covered his head. Seconds later, the rest of the ceiling collapsed inches away from where had just been laying.

The vibrating hull of the Mining Platform was deafening.

After a few moments, the intensity of the light from the great window began to fade, then was gone. The shuddering also subsided, then stopped.

Ryan crawled out from beneath one of the desks and looked around the deck for his comlink. In the confusion of the blast, he had dropped it, and now scrambled to find his only connection to the outside world. He found the comlink under a broken ceiling tile and brought it to his ear.

"Charlie, what the Hell happened?" he said into the receiver.

The comlink returned nothing but static. He switched to another channel and tried his call again.

"Bradford! Goddamnit! Damage report!"

"Terrorist attack…blew out the main reactor core," the voice replied in between pauses of static. "We're losing altitude…going down…too fast…unable to restart rotation…"

"Get everyone into the lifepods and get to safety."

"No time…dropping like a rock and…fail to get the electromagnetic field back on line…start the rotation again…twenty minutes…all going to die…"

"Charlie! Charlie!" he shouted.

But the comlink surrendered to static. He tried switching to another frequency, but he could not restore the connection.

Ryan was so consumed with trying to re-establish communication with his Administrative Assistant that he didn't notice an enormous shape as it emerged from the vast ocean of dense gas. Cloud Dancer, obscured partially by the clouds, floated up past the observation window and lingered for a moment.

Ryan gasped, awestruck.

None of the words or detailed drawings in Takahashi's report had even hinted at the sheer size or elegance of the alien lifeform. Ryan estimated it to be roughly one hundred feet in length, and though shaped like a hot-air balloon that was continually expanding and contracting, he likened the Jovian to a great blue whale. He watched as it rose toward the Platform, gathering small organisms and gas through a row of fringed plates in its mandible, much like a whale straining krill through its baleen. It glided up and past the window, all the while pumping its body up like some magnificent bodybuilder. Then, with several rhythmic contractions, the alien lifeform expelled both waste and gas from a rear exhaust and went sailing into the clouds by jet propulsion. A moment later, hundreds of meters away, its majestic body—now slender and elongated—broke through the clouds. It floated for an instant on a warm updraft, then dove back down to repeat the cycle again.

Ryan half expected such a tremendous lifeform to be clumsy and sluggish, but it moved like a graceful ballerina executing several leaps and turns in one, light flowing movement. The Jovian flitted across the tops of several clouds, like a great dancer, then plunged back down toward the surface.

"Cloud Dancer," he said to himself.

As the Jovian again passed by the window, Ryan took particular note of its colorization and markings. He saw that Cloud Dancer, while mostly beige in color, had several gray longitudinal furrows that ran along its streamlined body. And though its skin was smooth and hairless, he observed a row of small, stiff bristles near its crown. Neither of these features seemed to serve any purpose he could readily explain but they might be used in the future for identification purposes. He made a mental note to tell Yukiko when she was fully conscious.

Cloud Dancer was soon joined by a second one of its kind, then a third. As they glided past the viewing window, Ryan had the strange sensation that he was being watched by them. Like he was the one on display, being observed and having his seemingly purposeless features recorded for some future identification. The thought sent his mind reeling. He staggered back away from the window and put the palms of both hands to his head.

"What's going on?" he said aloud.

Ryan felt quite strange. He tried to shake off the feeling, dismissing his slight disorientation as the result of the high concentration of nitrogen gas that was still lingering in the chamber. The Pilot of the *Montgolfier* had warned him about the effects of the gas, but at that moment, he couldn't remember a damn thing she told him. His mind was suddenly spinning out of his head. He felt confused, light-headed, and it took every effort just to keep from losing his balance. But the more he struggled to maintain that balance, the more the dizziness intensified.

"What's happening to me?" he asked, not expecting anyone to answer.

Ryan was losing control of himself. One moment, he could feel the muscles in his lower limbs tighten in response to a message sent from the brain to keep his legs from buckling, and the next, they were twitching and moving at commands that were not wholly his own. He fought the urge to fall, but eventually succumbed to a force that was far greater than his own. Then he attempted to roll over on his side, but discovered that he could not seem to move another muscle. Looking down at his right hand, he tried to focus on closing the fingers into a fist. But this simple task became an ordeal of unimaginable proportions as well. He struggled with each finger, but soon realized the futility of his actions. He choked down a couple of breaths, his lungs laboring like a climber on Mt. Everest, then stared with unblinking eyes at the ceiling. He could no longer move on his own.

"No, this can't be happening …"

Within moments, the last ounce of feeling in his body had gone, and all that remained was a consciousness that seemed to drift in and out of reality. Ryan knew that he was laying helpless on the deck in the forward observation chamber, but his mind told him he was inching toward the edge of some great precipice. He struggled within himself to keep back, away from the edge, by trying to concentrate on things around him. First, he tried counting ceiling tiles, then he traced the outline of the fluorescent light fixtures with his eyes. But his mind kept returning him to that damned precipice.

"Noooooooooooooo!!!!!!!!!!!!"

Finally, he simply gave in and looked out into the dark abyss that lay before him. For all its unperceived depth, Ryan might well have been looking right into a black hole, or worse, the very bowels of Hell. His mind screamed in horror at the thought. Then, as if in slow motion, he found himself plunging downward. Tumbling head over foot, he tried to grasp at something—anything that would break his fall—but his limbs did not respond. He just continued plummeting further and further into darkness. . .

Beyond Time and Space

0

. . . and at last, there is only darkness.

Mitchell Ryan's eyes flutter open, and he is only dimly aware of his passage into some other time and place that has none of the linear sensibilities that he has come to rely upon to measure his reality. He seizes hold of the moment, fearful that he will loose all manner of perspective, but as he tightens his grasp, the moment has already fleeted away and been replaced by another. The notions of past and present and future all fold into one that his mind cannot seem to comprehend. He is becoming, all at once, a child and a man and a senior with no sense of beginning or ending, and in the wink of an eye, Ryan is as he has always been. He has passed beyond any reckoning of time and space to an infinite point that is the edge of eternity. Back on Earth, Mitchell's life was measured by clocks and calendars, holidays and anniversaries, graduations, weddings and funerals, births and deaths—the prevarications of a finite mind incapable of seeing time and space in any other manner. Only now does his mind begin to grasp the true complexity of the universe, and it squashes his ego. Perhaps the Jovians are lifeforms that live in the moment without any sense of past or future.

Then, as his eyes begin to adjust to the darkness, Ryan sees something, not clear at first, but something vague, formless. Gradually the image clears, and he observes a man bending down on one knee to comfort a child that is crying. He looks closer at the image and sees himself reflected in the man. He is that man, or rather was that man, for he no longer feels connected to the image. The child is Hiroki Takahashi, and the incident seems borrowed from his recent past. Ryan is aware that he is viewing the image now as some distant third party. But he is doing more than just viewing the image; he is also experiencing the strong emotional feelings that were part of that moment. He imagines himself as Ebenezer Scrooge taking the journey with the three Christmas ghosts in Charles Dickens' classic. Feelings of fear and loss, love and hope overwhelm him, and Ryan starts weeping as he is lifted to another plane, also beyond his ken.

He becomes aware of something just beyond his grasp and reaches out to touch it. Without warning, several hundred other images deluge his mind at once. They surge into his consciousness, and he tries assimilating each and every image as it unfolds. Ryan sees two friends holding each other in loving embrace...and witnesses that moment between Yukiko and Masaki Shibata. The image fades and is replaced in the wink of an eye by a new image of two adversaries arguing ethics...and Ryan is again in that moment with Reinhardt. That image fades and is replaced by one of a small boy cowering in fear under his blankets with his mother beside him...and he sees Yukiko and her son Hiroki. That image fades and is replaced by one of a man and a woman talking in the corridor of the Space Station...and he sees Rachel and Lenny Provenzo. Again, the image fades and is replaced by one of a crowd of people responding to a speaker with their applause…and Ryan feels the adoration of the crowd one more time. Next, he sees two aeronauts, Scott Glenn and Hiroki Takahashi, aboard the *Explorer II* airship…and he witnesses mankind's first close encounter with the Jovians. The images come and go in rapid succession, and with each one, a different emotion is experienced by Ryan. For one, he is crying; for another, he is angry; and yet for another, he is happy. The images flood his senses with sounds and shapes, smells and tastes, thoughts and feelings that are all distinctly human. The sensations fill him to the point of bursting; then, with one mighty discharge, he releases them all.

Instantly he grows lighter, freer. Ryan is no longer human; he has exchanged his physical form with one of the lifeforms, and now soars above the Jovian clouds just like one of them.

One moment, he floats above a warm updraft over the gas giant, and the next, he is dancing from cloud to cloud without a care in the world. He is still Ryan, but he is also Cloud Dancer. Together, Ryan tastes a familiar delight from childhood, and savors that intense feeling of living just for the moment. But as he turns his gaze toward the heavens and spies the first Voyager probe, his feeling of intense joy is quickly replaced by one of apprehension. Feelings of fear and loss, desperation and hopelessness wash over his new body and begin to swallow him whole. Even though he still retains the instincts of his alien host to float, Ryan's human thoughts struggle to keep him aloft. But the harder he tries on his own, the deeper he sinks.

Cloud Dancer whispers an incredibly powerful, yet simple command for him to 'relax'. He does not hear the message with ears, but rather with his entire physical being. Ryan is no longer afraid. The peace and absolute tranquillity of the Jovian's thoughts gradually fill him with a sense of friendship and good will. He stops struggling and is, at once, supported and sustained by several fellow lifeforms. They lift him up toward the heavens, rocking him gently. The sensation is pleasant, nurturing, and he grows lighter in their loving embrace. He feels he could stay here forever.

After a few moments or what could be a million years, he is again soaring high above the clouds. Ryan savors the moment, drinking in the pure and simple joy of being, but the moment is short lived. Once again, Ryan is aware of his human form as he and Cloud Dancer go zooming off in space.

There is no real sense of forward motion, but Ryan reacts like he is falling through some great hole in the cosmos that has opened up solely to swallow him and Cloud Dancer. He puts his hands out in front of him and twists his body to the left and right to level himself, but he cannot find a position in space that is comfortable. As far as he can trust his senses, Ryan appears to be dropping vertically. He is moving faster and faster, but the distant end of space never seems to change perspective. It remains forever constant. Only the stars seem to move, at first slowly, then at speeds that far exceed his ability to comprehend.

"Oh, my God," he says, his words stretching to infinity, resounding, echoing in the infinite reaches of time and space.

Ryan and Cloud Dancer are now traveling faster than the speed of light; trillions and trillions of miles flash by them in the blind of an eye. Stars, moons, planets, solar systems, then whole galaxies swirl past them in a kaleidoscope of colors never before imagined by man. Whirlpools of gas, glittering ice crystals, and pillars of fire hurtle by Ryan and Cloud Dancer at inconceivable speeds. Then odd shapes, that look vaguely familiar, rush towards them and race on by.

Ryan can hardly contain himself; he is overwhelmed, awed and humbled by the experience.

Ryan and Cloud Dancer are emerging from a tunnel now. The far end of space, which had seemed so distant to him moments before, is coming closer, and steadily widening before him, filling his point of view. The stars towards the center are winking out of existence, but only Ryan seems to notice as the two move closer and closer to the end.

"The stars! They're vanishing," he cries out, but his words are not heard.

Then there is nothing but blackness. It is a dark void without any shape or depth. There are no stars. There is no sound, just an unimaginable cacophony of silence. From his perspective, Ryan cannot make out any distinctive features. There are no familiar objects by which he can judge the size or scale of things. He reaches out with his hands to orient himself in space, but he cannot determine which way is up and which way is down. He tries again and again, but he becomes frustrated by the whole process and finally stops.

Ryan then sees something in the distance. He is not quite sure what it is, but points it out to Cloud Dancer. The Jovian does not respond to him.

"Look!" he shouts.

They have traveled back in time, fifteen to twenty billions years ago, when the entirety of the universe was compressed into the confines of a single atomic nucleus. Ryan and Cloud Dancer are observers looking at that moment before creation when time and space does not exist. They are looking at a small, subatomic particle, a singularity which will explode and become the Universe.

Ryan and the Jovian are floating in the void, watching and waiting for something to happen. Ryan is the first to notice it. He screams at the top of his lungs, but there is no air to carry his voice. Cloud Dancer does not hear him. He continues to shout again and again:

"It's shrinking. It's shrinking."

Cloud Dancer does not react to his cry, but Ryan knows what he has seen and keeps watching. It is actually happening. The singularity is growing smaller. The atomic nucleus is shrinking in size. And as the size gets smaller, the brightness of the singularity is fading.

Ryan is transfixed by what is happening. His eyes are filled with a combination of awe and wonder. Ryan knows that he is witnessing an event that is so spectacular…and so far beyond the scope of human understanding…that this mind can only barely comprehend it. He is witnessing the birth of the Universe.

"Let there be light," he whispers to himself.

And then, there is a blinding flash. The flash is of a size and brilliance that no one has ever imagined, and it blinds him, temporarily. Ryan tries to turn his head away, tries to shield his eyes with the palms of his hands, but he is too late. The blinding flash is so intense and so truly spectacular that he can only see white before his eyes. The dark black void, already a distant memory, is now all white. In fact, everything around Ryan has turned a brilliant white…

Saturday
Evening

40

Still blinded by what he saw, Ryan stumbled forward with his hands outstretched in front of him to feel the way. At first, he imagined that he was still back in the timeless void, trapped between the Big Bang and the formation of the universe; but then, as his other senses began to register familiar data, he realized that he had returned to the forward compartment of the Mining Platform. He smelled a cup of coffee that had soured at someone's workstation; he heard the sound of ventilation flowing through the ducts over head, and felt the cool rush of re-circulated air on his face. Under his feet, he felt the solid deck. Ryan felt like a modern-day Tiresias, that Greek prophet of classical mythology, who had been shown the great mysteries of the universe only to be struck blind by the gods.

Blinking his eyes, he rotated his memory through the color spectrum from reds to yellows to greens to blues. He drifted through the dense fog of remembrance, trying to recall even the simplest of things, and he struggled to make odd shapes into concrete images that he knew and recognized. He blinked again and again, and with each blink, his surroundings gradually came into focus. In time, he stared in absolute astonishment at the world that he had so long taken for granted. Recognition did wonders for his condition. The sudden remembrance shot a mega-dose of adrenaline into his system and made his pulse quicken.

Ryan then changed his focus and looked down at his arms and legs, feeling the life that coursed back into his veins. He focused on his right hand and ordered his fingers to close into a fist; they answered without hesitation. Then he focused on the fingers of his left hand and they responded as well. He stomped his feet on the deck and felt secure on solid ground. He was alive, and he smiled to himself, realizing what an awesome gift the Jovians had given him. At long last, Ryan felt renewed and at peace with himself, as if he had been living his entire existence in the darkness and was now able to see the light.

He glanced up at the circular window and his gaze settled on Cloud Dancer, who was floating just beyond reach. Ryan did not react with fear, but merely smiled with understanding.

He reached toward the window, slowly enough so that his actions would not be mistaken as hostile. Cloud Dancer hovered motionless. Ryan put both hands on the Plexiglas and felt vibrations on its cool surface. Feelings of good will and friendship seemed to radiate from the Jovian right through the window.

He stared at the alien lifeform for a while longer, then opened his mouth to speak, but nothing came out.

Ryan's mind had gone blank. *What do I say*, he thought, his eyes traveling up and down the length of the Jovian's body. The Chief Administrator felt disappointed in himself. He had never been at a loss for words throughout his entire political career; but now, at the very moment of first contact with a completely new species of intelligent life, he couldn't think of anything to say.

"Hello, how are you doing?" he said haltingly, tripping over each syllable. "My name is…" Ryan stopped, mortified by his assumption the Jovians could speak English. He stared back at Cloud Dancer, wondering how he was supposed to communicate directly with it.

Almost at once, he knew; he didn't know how he knew, he simply knew. Just as humans communicated with one another through words, the Jovians communicated through images. Not random images, he reasoned, but rather with images that conveyed some kind of emotional response. At first, their images must have been simple ones to convey the simple joy of being; but as the Jovian lifeforms began encountering the first human explorers and engineers, they incorporated these new images to communicate their strong emotional reactions. He suspected their first glimpse of an Earth probe must have become a universal image for fear and apprehension. Other images, like his encounter with Hiroshi in the docking bay or his argument with Reinhardt or Yukiko's need for a hug from Shibata, also helped expand their 'vocabulary' for the inevitable first contact with humans.

Nodding his head, Ryan turned away from the creature in embarrassment. He was the biggest fool in the world not to realize they couldn't communicate with him in a manner most humans found conventional. It was clear that he would have to adopt their unusual method of expression if he wanted to communicate with them.

He closed his eyes, cutting off all visual distractions from the outside, and focused on a familiar image in his mind that would convey greeting. He then ransacked his feelings for the single emotion connected with "hello." Initially, the creature did not respond to his message; but as Ryan struggled to perfect the image and get it right, Cloud Dancer returned in kind.

"We were so wrong about you," he said through the glass, knowing the Jovian could not hear his words, but hoping it would comprehend his meaning. "I was so wrong about you."

At long last, Mitchell Ryan guessed the Jovian lifeforms had been trying to initiate first contact for some time, but he and the others had been either too stupid or too arrogant to notice. He figured they probably began watching humans from a distance, waiting for just the right opportunity to come calling. Once the Space Station had been built and the Mining Platform was nearing completion, one or two of them likely tried to communicate with humans. Apparently, they may have even thought the scientists on the Platform were manifesting images in return, for they continued with their efforts. But the Jovian lifeforms probably mistook the human's cold, scientific probes as an exchange of some kind. He could just imagine their frustration at trying to assimilate the probes and failing to get a proper response. Ryan's own instructions to gather hard empirical data was ultimately what drove them away. He nodded at the Jovian, which was still hovering beyond the window

"Cloud Dancer, your kind has been here for billions of years, a great deal longer than man has walked on Earth, and you were just trying to extend a little Jovian hospitality when we noisy trespassers barged into your quiet neighborhood," Ryan said, his face turning red with both shame and embarrassment. "How we must have seemed to you, like the primitive apes that we are, blundering into your paradise with all of our noisy equipment and blustery self-importance. We never even asked you if it was okay. Your collective memory that stretches back to the very beginning of time itself must have thought that we had quite the nerve, for I am certain that no other species you may have encountered over the long years had been as presumptuous. How could we have been so eager to destroy you, just to satisfy our own selfish needs, when you are so much more evolved than us?"

Cloud Dancer did not respond to him. The Jovian had difficulty following the human's syntax, while Ryan found himself relying on the images he recalled from his waking dream rather than trying to create new ones. In the end, he hoped that his sense of humility and sincerity would be enough to convey his meaning.

"You are the caretakers of the universe, and we are just some poor tenants who happen to occupy one of its many worlds. You'll be here long after my civilization has fallen back to dust, if we don't destroy you first with our own greed. You are the essence of creation…"

Ryan paused for a moment. His face had gone blank. He took a deep breath into his lungs and slowly exhaled without any conscious thought, struggling to pull it all together neatly in his own mind. Even though they communicated in a uniquely separate way and were worlds apart ideologically, he somehow sensed the Jovians were more like humans than different. They may have actually needed one another more than either was willing to admit.

"No, it goes much deeper than that, doesn't it?" he asked.

With unblinking eyes, Mitchell Ryan looked to Cloud Dancer for a response, but the Jovian remained silent, hovering motionless on the other side of the Plexiglas. Ryan's eyes reflected the glare from the glowing light in front and all around him. Then, that look of dawning revelation filled his face with a brightness that was far more intense than the light from a hundred stars.

"You and I…we're both part of that creation…"

Ryan stared back through the glass at Cloud Dancer with incredible awe. He tried to conjure an image from Sunday school class of God and Creation, but before it was fully formed in his mind, Ryan's gentle snapshot was met with a barrage of images, most of which he could not even begin to understand. Again, his mind was sent reeling, as these abstract concepts took form in bizarre and unusual shapes that his own limited imagination could hardly grasp.

"But we're more than just a product of creation. We are the creator made flesh and blood," he babbled, the words tumbling without sense out of his mouth. "We are the creator and the created...forever joined to give the universe form and substance. We are all one."

Cloud Dancer rocked back and forth, as if to acknowledge in some way Ryan's very crude understanding of a much larger truth that the Jovians had known for millions upon millions of years. Ryan smiled with relief. His head felt like it was going to blow off his shoulders at any moment, but at last, he understood. Then he stared down at his comlink, and his face filled instantly with terror. Mere moments had passed in the space of time, and in those moments Ryan was lost to the Jovians. But now he was aware, very aware, of the impending doom.

"The Station..." he whispered.

He glanced up at Cloud Dancer and put his hands up to the Plexiglas.

"Cloud Dancer...how can I make you aware that I need your help. Can you read my thoughts? Do you know the emotions I am feeling? My Station is in trouble...and I need your help."

He attempted to make his meaning clear to Cloud Dancer by motioning to the Jovian. Then he squeezed his eyes closed and tried to project his thoughts with the fingers of both hands held at his temples and his head to the glass. But Cloud Dancer remained motionless.

"You've got to help me."

41

Hundreds of kilometers away, the Space Station was flooded with fear and panic as the residents, guests and Station personnel struggled to get to safety before it dropped into the abyss of Jupiter. In one section, people streamed down the narrow corridors like ants to the Central Core, carrying boxes and personal items. In another, panicking people were hurdled against the bulkhead and trampled each other to the floor as several aftershocks erupted and buffeted the Station wildly. In yet another section, a woman cowered in a dark corner, holding one of her children in her arms and shielding the other with her body. Her two children were crying aloud in terror, but their cries were muffled by the screams of those racing by. And in the docking bay, the dock workers scrambled to ready the small number of escape pods and were suddenly overrun by people racing to be the first to escape.

*   *   *   *   *

Just outside the administrative suites, Bradford stood in the corridor directing people, like a traffic cop, to the docking bay. He was sobbing and tears had stained his dark alabaster features. He tried to maintain order with his well-rehearsed use of hand signs and traffic signals, but he was fighting a losing battle. The fear and panic of mob rule had overtaken all manner of reason. Finally, he himself was swept up in the flood of humanity and pulled down the corridor.

*   *   *   *   *

Rachel scrambled into her quarters. She threw a handful of personal belongings, including Lenny's baseball cap, into a bag and headed back to the door. She paused for a moment, then pulled a folded letter out of her pocket. It was addressed to Mitchell Ryan. She smoothed the letter out and placed it on the nightstand beside her bed. Then she turned back to the door and ran into the stream of fleeing residents.

*   *   *   *   *

In sickbay, Doctor Rudenko and several Medical Technicians were helping to administer the wounds of the injured Station personnel, as still more poured through the double doors from the corridor.

Clad only in a bra and panties, Takahashi floated upright in a vertical position inside the hyberbaric chamber, with a set of electrodes attached to key spots on her chest. The Medical Technician who had helped to bring her back to life was attending her from the other side of the glass, aided by two nurses. He monitored her heartbeat and breathing, while the other two gradually increased the air pressure one atmosphere at a time. They hoped that by increasing the partial pressure of oxygen her blood would gradually be oxygenated. For a while it appeared as if she were trying to resist the urge to breathe normally, preferring short, irregular breaths instead. Though unconscious, her body still trashed about in delirium.

Nearby, Suki Takahashi comforted her grandson Hiroki by holding him close to her and stroking his hair. His was crying his eyes out, and with each new explosion, he shuddered in fear.

*   *   *   *   *

At the docking bay, Cramden and his Security Team had taken over from the dock workers and were fighting to maintain order. But each time a new escape pod was maneuvered into place by the forklifts overhead, a mass of Station personnel and residents raced up the ramp, pushing and shoving to be first to climb in, under a hail of explosions and blinding sparks. Cramden tried to hold them back, but he was knocked to the ground and trampled under foot.

Just then, as if nothing else could go wrong, the Station began to rock back and forth, like a top spinning out of control.

Bloodied and battered, the Security Chief crawled to one side and collapsed.

42

Mitchell Ryan pounded on the Plexiglas with both hands, pleading, "You've got to help me! Hundreds of lives are at stake! If you and I are indeed one in the same creation, then we're got to learn to work together. We've got to make certain that every life—Jovian and Terran—is sacred."

Without warning, Cloud Dancer moved away from the observation window, expelling both waste and gas from a rear exhaust. The Jovian went sailing into the clouds by jet propulsion.

"No! Don't leave!" Ryan cried out in horror as he watched the alien soar away. "You've got to stay and help me!"

Not that far away, but well out Ryan's view, Cloud Dancer glided purposely through the great idle herd of Jovian lifeforms floating in the warm updraft near the Mining Platform. Most of the Jovians ignored him; some who were simply content to graze like cattle on the tiniest of organic molecules even turned away so that they did not have to acknowledge his presence among them. The few that did take notice turned to greet him as he passed.

Cloud Dancer propelled himself forward at a steady, even pace, electrostatic discharges pulsing from his crown as he moved. The discharges, like flashes of lightning during a violent thunderstorm, struck several of his fellow Jovians who, in turn, replied with their own flashes of lightning. Had Ryan witnessed the exchange, he would have been convinced they were talking to each other, using thought projections of pure energy instead of words and phrases.

Suddenly, without any kind of warning, six Jovians broke away from the herd and propelled themselves upward, towards the cooler regions of Jupiter's atmosphere. Each of them tried pumping harder, gliding further, and traveling faster than the others, fighting to be the first but then dropping back into the pack as another one of the six took the lead. The lead changed hands several times as each one of the six Jovians took turns racing in front of the pack through the clouds.

Then, finally, one emerged as the clear favorite and took a substantial lead over the other five. Its majestic body—one moment, long and slender, and the next, pumped up like an Olympian god—charged forward. But as the Jovian struggled to climb higher and higher in the stratosphere, its forward momentum began to slow down. It became sluggish, and slowed to a crawl. Then it exploded, sending particles and debris flying in its wake.

The other five Jovians rushed to feed on their fallen comrade's carcass, like frenzied piranha in a South American rainforest, devouring every last particle in seconds. With renewed energy and vitality, they continued moving upward, propelling themselves faster and faster.

A few of the lighter and faster Jovians broke through to the higher, cooler layers, expanding and contracting the planetary gases, while the others plodded along. Each one of them seemed to be reaching for the stars themselves as they struggled against all odds to each the Station and space itself.

* * * * *

Ryan had managed to swing the Platform's telescope around so he could bring the image of the Space Station into frame. He flicked a few buttons on the central monitor and watched as the Station came into focus. Even though he could not be with his personnel during this moment of crisis, Ryan was bound and determined to watch over them until the very end. He also knew that their demise meant his inevitable doom as no one would be coming to save him. He had no way of knowing the Jovians were fighting their way to the Station.

From his perspective, he watched as the Space Station rolled back and forth in the upper cloud stratum, like a mighty sea vessel that had struck an iceberg and was floundering in an endless succession of swells. He could see that the lights in its towering spires had grown dark, and the only sign of life was the orange glow that radiated from the nuclear reactor core. He also spotted a small flotilla of ships and escape craft bobbing in and out of the clouds nearby.

43

The corridor outside the sickbay had grown quiet and was dimly lit by the emergency lights. A single Medical Technician carrying supplies hurried down the corridor past one of the observation windows.

Just then, some movement outside the window caught his eyes. The reflection of the emergency lights in the glass obscured his view for an instant, but as he drew nearer the window, he witnessed a monstrous chunk of protoplasm emerging from the dense clouds below and heading towards the Station.

Startled, he dropped his supplies and raced around the corner towards sickbay.

*   *   *   *   *

In the upper reaches of the stratosphere, a single Jovian approached the Space Station with caution. The alien lifeform discharged several electrostatic pulses at the central core in an attempt to communicate.

* * * * *

The dull lights in sickbay went bright for a second, then flickered out, and finally came back on, brighter than ever. Each time the lights went out, there was a collective gasp as the Doctors, Nurses, Technicians and patients took a deep breath seemingly at the same time, then released it in an audible sigh as the lights came back on.

Rudenko glanced up at the ceiling lights. "What the Hell…"

The frightened Medical Technician rushed into the operating theater just as Rudenko was about to return to his patient.

"There's something out there," the Tech said, nearly out of breath.

"Where?" Rudenko asked, with skepticism.

"Outside the Station."

"That's impossible!"

Suddenly, the Station was rocked by a sudden impact, and every single electrical system in the sickbay snapped to life with a spike of energy. Everyone in the Medical Center reacted in their own individual ways, but the general consensus among the Doctors, Nurses and patients was that they were living on borrowed time. At any moment, they expected the end.

"There it is! Listen! Listen!" the Medical Technician cried.

Near the door, among those who had just been delivered to sickbay, Cramden looked up from his gurney and moaned.

"I've got to get to my post," he said, nearly delirious.

Rudenko raced over to his side and held him down. "You're not going anywhere," he ordered. "Whatever this is, we can't be any worse off than we already are."

"But…"

Before Cramden could utter another word, Rudenko

grabbed a sedative and pumped him full of the contents of the syringe. Then he glanced up at the ceiling and paused to ponder their predicament. His reverie was cut short by his Medical Technician.

"We're all going to die!" he shouted in panic.

Rudenko slapped him across his face. "Pull yourself together, man!" he demanded. "We've got patients who need our help!"

"What difference does it make? We're all going to die anyway."

"No one dies," Rudenko shouted at the top of his lungs so that everyone could hear him, "unless I say they do!"

All of the Medical Personnel and a few of the patients lying on gurneys were stunned by his outburst and stopped what they were doing. As several seconds ticked off the clock, the tension in the room was so thick that a surgeon could cut it with a scalpel. No one moved, or even dared to breathe. Finally, Rudenko looked sternly around the room at each and every one of his people and eased the tension with a nod of confidence. Almost at once, they were back to work.

"I sent you out of here for supplies," Rudenko scowled at the Medical Technician. "Where are they?'

"I dropped them in the hall, sir," he replied, in a whisper.

"Well, go get them! And fast!"

The Chief Medical Officer watched the Tech race out of sickbay, then stared back at the ceiling.

*   *   *   *   *

The single Jovian had wrapped himself around the Central Core of the Space Station and struggled with Herculean intensity to stabilize its out-of-control spiraling descent. Several other Jovians approached with caution, but after a moment's hesitation, they attached themselves to other key sections of the

Station's longitudinal axis. Its rotation began to slow and the wobble of its axis steadied.

*   *   *   *   *

For an instant, the Space Station shuddered. People and equipment were knocked to the ground. Parts of the overhead conduit broke loose and sparks from the emergency lights rained down from the ceiling.

After a few seconds, the shuddering began to subside, then stopped.

One by one, the Station personnel and residents started to look up at the overhead bulkhead, and the reality that they had survived began to dawn collectively on their faces. Among them, Bradford searched for other members of his staff. One was laying on the floor next to him. They acknowledged each other with a smile, for there was nothing much more to say. Every one of them were confounded and surprised by the unexpected turn of events.

44

Ryan had been watching the events unfold on the central monitor and simply could not believe his eyes. He pushed a series of buttons and the image on the monitor clicked from its current view to closer and closer ones. When telescope had delivered its closest view, Ryan saw four Jovians wrapped around the body of the Station like swaddling cloth around an infant. With his mouth wide open, he gaped at the monitor in utter disbelief. His face was red; his eyes were puffy, and tears of joy were running down his cheeks.

"I don't believe it," he repeated over and over again. "I just don't believe it."

After a few moments, he turned away from the monitor and stared out the forward observation window. The lumbering herd of Jovians had moved away and all that he could see were the clouds of Jupiter's atmosphere. He strained against the glass, but Cloud Dancer was nowhere to be seen.

"Thank you, Cloud Dancer," he said to himself.

Not far from the Mining Platform, but still out of visual range, Cloud Dancer reacted to Ryan's words and feelings of gratitude by soaring back into the atmosphere and breaching through the clouds. For an instant of total joy, the Jovian glided on a warm updraft, then plunged back down into the clouds.

Sunday

45

Several hours later, Ryan opened the air lock, his face illuminated by the bank of red warning lights. With all the chaos and excitement aboard the Station, the airship *Icarus* had taken its time to return to the Mining Platform and Ryan was starting to get anxious about returning home. He pulled the weighty hatch back and latched it to the bulkhead. All of a sudden, a large man with a knife lunged through the opening and sliced Ryan across the lapel of his suit. Instantly, Ryan pivoted on the ladder, using the weightlessness to his advantage, and dropped to the deck below, landing with both feet under him, ready to move.

Climbing hand over hand, with the knife between his teeth like a modern-day pirate, the Assassin scurried down the ladder headfirst. Ryan was waiting for him at the bottom and used the man's sudden weight gain, as he moved from the weightless environment to gravity, to good advantage. He grabbed the Assassin at the middle rung and hurled him across the room with what appeared to be superhuman strength. The man thudded against the wall of the docking bay, but rolled to one side, shifting the knife from between his teeth to his left hand.

The Assassin lunged again, slashing Ryan's arm with the knife as he struggled to his feet. Ryan was momentarily stunned as he felt his arm, then looked down at the blood on his hand.

"Who are you? Why are you doing this?"

The Assassin just looked straight through him, like he was in a trance. He appeared to be a man with a singular mission and would stop at nothing to kill Ryan. He lunged at Ryan again, but Ryan sidestepped his blow, spun around, and smashed the Assassin in the face with his fist. The man hit the deck.

"Okay…now, I want some answers." Ryan demanded, out of breath.

With flawless precision, the Assassin executed a perfect drop swipe at Ryan's feet and, as the Chief Administrator fell, the Assassin wrapped his legs around Ryan's neck and tried to snap it. Ryan struggled to get free, then found his own opening for attack. He hammered down with a single groin punch that stunned his assailant for a second, enabling him enough time to drum-roll his body of out of harm's way. Then Ryan scrambled to his feet and raced down the corridor in the direction of the forward compartment, followed closely by the Assassin.

Ryan charged down the narrow hall, scanning the shadows, looking for a weapon, any kind of weapon, to fight back. He was covered in blood, and the Assassin was just a few steps behind him.

All of a sudden, one of the shadows came alive. The Shadow Man stepped out of the darkness and struck Ryan's assailant across the back of his neck with a karate chop. The Assassin reacted by spinning around with the blade of his knife up, but he was far too slow for Shadow Man's cat-like reflexes. Shadow Man pivoted in place and struck a second, disabling blow to the assailant's upper chest cavity. The Assassin went down hard, his eyes folding back into his head.

With sweat pouring off his face, Ryan looked at Shadow Man and smiled.

"Thanks," he said, breathless. "I thought he had me."

"Not a chance, Mister Ryan," Shadow Man replied. "I've been following your every movement the last several days. I should have anticipated the ambush at the air lock. Sorry"

"Didn't I fire you?"

"Yes, but under the circumstance…"

"Well," Ryan said, with a shrug, "consider yourself back on the payroll."

"Thank you, sir."

"No, I'm the one who should be thanking you,…" Ryan fumbled with Shadow Man's first name. "Just what the Hell is your name, anyway?"

"John," he said simply.

"John?"

"Just John."

"Well, okay, 'John,'" Ryan said, with a grin, "I hope you've been briefed on piloting an airship. I'd like to get back to the Station."

"Yes, sir."

46

The docking bay looked like a twisted mess of metal, wires and equipment, but dock workers and other Station personnel were already hard at work removing the wreckage and trying to restore order to the chaos. People were still disembarking from the cargo ships and escape pods.

One at a time, Ryan and the others were helped out of the airlock by men wearing orange fatigues. John, the Shadow Man, shoved the Assassin forward, but kept a steady hold on his left arm like a dog on a very short leash. Ryan struggled to climb to his feet, and once he reached firm ground, he took several deep gulps of air, drinking in the rich oxygen and other gases of the Station. His wounds, which were largely superficial, had already stopped bleeding.

Bradford and Cramden were there to greet them. Cramden steadied himself with a cane. The Security Chief still looked pretty badly battered, his head bandaged and his arm in a sling.

"Welcome back," Bradford said, warmly shaking hands with Ryan. "I see you've met 'John.'"

"Yes," Ryan replied. "He saved my life."

"It was a life worth saving," John added.

Ryan groaned. "But the next time I catch you doing something sneaky like this…"

"I guess I owe you an explanation," Bradford offered.

"…you'll be looking for a new assignment."

"Understood."

Ryan looked at each of the three people gathered around him during the long, uncomfortable pause. He rubbed his days-old beard, then his face broke out in a big, wide grin.

"By the way," Ryan said, patting Bradford on the back, "you did okay here. I'm really proud of you, Charlie."

"Thank you, sir, but I really can't take any of the credit," his assistant replied. "The Jovians…they…"

"Yes, I know. They're a pretty miraculous species."

"The casualty count is mercifully low, and thanks to the Jovians, we'll have the Station back to operation by the end of the week," Bradford concluded.

"Well done," he added, then turned to Cramden. "What happened to you?"

"It's just a scratch, sir," the Security Chief replied, hiding the cane from view. "I already feel like I'm getting my second wind."

Ryan pointed to the Assassin and said, "Cramden, I think you'll find this is the man who killed Shibata and Provenzo, and undoubtedly planted the bomb that took out the reactor core."

Cramden signaled to two of his men to take charge of the Assassin. Relieved, John released his hold on the prisoner and stepped back as Cramden moved in for a closer inspection.

"So, he's the Martian terrorist?"

"No, he's a paid political assassin," Ryan corrected him. "There's no revolution on Mars, just a handful of rich, old men who want us to think so."

"What?" Bradford interjected.

"That's crazy," Cramden added.

"I know it sounds insane," Ryan admitted, "but there's a man locked in one of the VR centers who can verify all of this."

The Security Chief paused for a moment to search his memory. So much had happened in the last twenty-four hours that he had almost forgotten the man his team had found.

"Edward Reinhardt?" Cramden asked.

"Yes…"

"Edward Reinhardt was found dead in Virtual Reality Center Five," he reported, as a matter of fact. "Apparently, a heart attack. My men found his body sprawled over the emergency shutdown switch. The panel was broken."

Ryan shot Cramden a surprised look.

Bradford added, "We think he was trying out an advanced mountain climbing program, somehow got confused, disoriented, and tried to shut down the simulation. In his eagerness to stop the program, he must have broken the switch instead. Died right there on the spot, without every reaching the door."

Ryan took a deep breath and sighed. He was obviously shaken by the news, but Bradford and Cramden did not press him for details. The news disturbed him greatly, and yet, at the same time, he couldn't help but feel a sense of release, much like a mistreated slave who had just learned that his master was dead.

"What would you like me to do with the body, sir?" his assistant asked.

"I'll notify his next of kin," Ryan mumbled.

"That's your prerogative, Mister Ryan."

The Chief Administrator turned to Cramden. "Take this man down to interrogation," he said, pointing at the assassin. "I want a complete list of his contacts and whereabouts for the last forty-eight months."

"You'll never make me talk," the Assassin said.

Cramden got right in the man's face and barked, "We'll just see about that." Then he looked down at the Assassin's feet. "I've got a partial shoe print that should just match those shoes of yours."

"What?" the Assassin returned.

"Take him away, boys," Cramden said to his men, "and lock him up."

Ryan turned away from his Security Chief and nodded at Bradford. "Charlie, you're with me," he said, heading toward the corridor that connected with the Central Core, his assistant footsteps behind. "Listen. I need you to set up a meeting with the delegates from the United Planets."

"Mister Ryan," he said, "are you sure you want to do this?"

"I don't understand what you mean."

"Postpone the Platform's official opening on Monday, sir," he said, anticipating his boss's next move. Bradford seemed upset to Ryan, not agitated or angry, more anxious. "You could have a real public relations nightmare on your hand if there's any kind of delay."

Without turning his head, Ryan snarled, "I'm no longer concerned with what anyone else has to say. But if you're that worried about the press, draft an official policy statement and I'll look it over."

"What should I say?"

"I don't care," Ryan responded, throwing his arms into the air. "You're supposed to be my administrative assistant."

"But what if I get it wrong?"

"Mistakes are what make us human, Charlie," Ryan said, recalling Rudenko's words. "Never be afraid to be human."

"It's just that…" Bradford confessed, "I'm not a very good liar, Mister Ryan."

Ryan's stride hesitated, but he kept going. "I'll issue the statement myself some time tomorrow," he conceded, with a deep sigh.

"And the unions?"

Ryan strode on in silence.

"The unions will have to be told something," Bradford continued his litany of concerns. "They're not going to like being shut out on the first day of work. They'll expect to be fully compensated."

"I'll handle the unions."

Doggedly, Bradford followed Ryan through the heart of the Central Core. "I'm not sure that this is the right thing to do," he repeated. "Maybe you should take a moment to rethink this…"

Ryan swung around, grabbed Bradford by the lapels of his jacket, and shoved him against the bulkhead. "I know what I'm doing, Charlie," he snapped. "In fact, I've never been so sure in all of my life. The Jovians are sentient lifeforms, and they deserve the same considerations that we would extend any conscious being. If that means we have to negotiate with them for the rights to mine here, then we had better come up with an effective strategy."

Bradford stared at him, visibly shocked by his boss's abrupt action. "I guess you know what this really means," he stammered.

"No, why don't you explain it to me."

"If you're wrong…we'll both be out of a job," he replied, forcing a laugh.

Ryan loosened his rigid grip on Bradford's lapels and gradually lowered him to the deck. He brushed out the wrinkles in his aide's jacket with the palms of both hands. He couldn't begin to explain what had just come over him, and made no effort to apologize to him.

"I guess you're probably right," Ryan responded with a half smile, "but I'm not wrong."

Bradford nodded his head in agreement.

Ryan turned to continue down the corridor, then glanced back at his assistant. "If you need me, I'll be in sickbay," Ryan said as he turned away and left Bradford standing all alone in the corridor.

47

On his way to sickbay, Ryan stopped by Rachel's quarters to see how she had faired during the crisis. He had half-expected her to be waiting for him in the docking bay, and when she didn't show up, he started to worry about her. He entered her room, and looked around. Her quarters were in a shambles. Tables and chairs had been overturned; the mattress from her bed lay on its side, and personal belongings were scattered around the room. The room looked like it had been ransacked, but Ryan knew better than that.

"Rachel," he called for her. "Rachel…"

He continued to look for her and call her name as he moved through the room. He tried not disturb any of her personal belongings, and moved only those things that were directly in his way. Stepping close to the bed, he noticed an envelope, which had been folded, on the floor next to her nightstand. He picked it up and saw that it was addressed to him in her handwriting.

Without much deliberation, he grabbed a chair and turned it upright. He sat down and tore the envelope open with his hands. Inside was a one-page letter written to him.

"Dearest Mitchell, if you are reading this letter…" he read the letter to himself, hearing the words from her soft voice curl over her luscious lips. "…then that means you are safe, and have survived the terrorist attack on the Station. I've been promised a place on one of the first evacuation transports, and I plan to stay aboard for the return trip home, to Earth, where I belong."

In his mind, Ryan imagined that Rachel was safe aboard a cargo ship, looking out the observation portal with tears in her eyes, as it lumbered through Jovian space on its journey home to Earth.

"Please don't follow me or try to contact me," he continued reading her letter. "I love you very, very deeply, and perhaps always will, but I just could not bear to see that look of disappointment and sadness in your face when I told you 'goodbye,' and have taken the cowardly way out with this note."

He stared down at the letter, mumbling the words to himself, trying to hold back the flood of tears.

"I've done some truly wicked things, and I'm sorry. I tried to tell you last night, but I just couldn't find the right words. Please know that I never meant to hurt you, or put your life at risk," he nodded his head as he read. "You are the dearest, sweetest man I have ever known. Please, when you think about me, and I do hope that you will think about me often, don't judge me or my actions too harshly. Instead, think about those innocent days when we first met, and remember the woman that I was, for we will always have Paris. Love 'France.'"

Ryan crumpled the letter in his hands. Overwhelmed with grief, he looked like a man who had just had his heart ripped out. He bowed his head, as if to say a prayer, and started crying.

48

A Nurse and two Medical Technicians were conferring in the Station's infirmary when Ryan stepped through the door. He looked like he had been through Hell, and all three stopped talking long enough to stare at him, then resumed their conversation. Ryan continued into the room, walking straight up to the hyperbaric chamber. Young Hiroshi, who had been watching his mother with his face pressed up against the thick glass, turned in anticipation of his approach. Ryan playfully mussed the boy's hair, nodded at his grandmother Suki, then exhaled with relief at the site of Yukiko. She was still submerged in the chamber, but she was now alert and conscious. For a while it appeared as if she were trying to resist the urge to breathe normally, preferring short, irregular breaths instead. Then, at the sight of Ryan, she relaxed, succumbing to the new air.

From the other side of the chamber, Rudenko monitored her heartbeat and breathing, while two of his Medical Technicians gradually decreased the air pressure one atmosphere at a time. They hoped that, by decreasing the partial pressure of oxygen, her blood would gradually be oxygenated. Despite the many tons of pressure in the chamber enclosing her, the Japanese scientist was finally out of danger and on the road to recovery.

Rudenko glanced up from his instrument panel and angled his head toward Ryan, without looking directly at him. "Doctor Takahashi is responding well to the treatment," he reported without expression. "We should have her back to breathing at normal pressure in a couple of hours."

"Any sign of permanent lung damage?" Ryan asked.

"None whatsoever."

"Thanks, doc," he said, smiling. "That's one I owe you and your staff."

Rudenko finally looked at Ryan and was appalled by what he saw. "I better take a look at those wounds of yours," he insisted.

"In a moment, doc."

The Chief Medical Officer turned back to his beeping monitor.

Ryan pressed his face to the glass. He had not the slightest idea how the hyperbaric chamber worked, but he was convinced it could work miracles as he stared into the woman's face.

"*Ya, genki kai?*" Ryan asked her condition through the loud speaker.

Yukiko nodded that she was fine. She could not actually speak as she was submerged in a special liquid substance and breathed through tubes in her nose and mouth. She blinked her eyes to focus on Ryan.

"Please accept my humble apology. You were right all along about the Jovians," he said, then tried to repeat the words again in Japanese.

Yukiko shot Ryan a confused look that communicated more her surprise than confusion at what he said.

"I had an..." Ryan struggled to find the right word. "...an encounter with Cloud Dancer. It was truly amazing, and even now, I'm having trouble believing that it actually happened..."

She continued to look at him, surprised.

"...but I know it did," he added. "Suffice it to say, I'm going to need your help to convince the others that what we experienced with the Jovians wasn't some nitrogen-induced hallucination, but first contact with an alien species."

Yukiko nodded her head affirmatively.

"They are sentient lifeforms, with a far greater understanding and connection to the mystery of the universe than we could have ever imagined," Ryan continued, leaning on the glass of the chamber. "But more than that, they reminded me that we humans are a part of that mystery as well. That we are more than just carbon-based lifeforms. That we are luminous beings of pure thought and energy, forever joined together to give the universe form and substance."

She looked at Ryan without any expression.

"I know. I don't quite understand it all myself, but I'm willing to learn from the Jovians," Ryan confessed. "I think they will be our friends, if we don't destroy ourselves or them first, and together Terrans and Jovians can forge ahead and purge the darkness of our fear and ignorance."

Rudenko walked over to Ryan and put his right hand on his shoulder. "Save the speeches for your constituency, Senator," he said, half jokingly. "This is a hospital, not a political forum."

"Sorry, doc."

"Now, I've got a bed over here with your name on it."

"But…"

"No buts," the Medical Chief cut Ryan off, "or do I need to remind you that, in sickbay, I outrank everyone, including Senators."

"Understood," he replied, then turned back to Yukiko. "We'll talk more about this tomorrow." Ryan started to follow Rudenko, then said over his shoulder, "By the way, Yukiko, I know for a fact that your husband died a hero, attempting to make first contact with the Jovians."

Yukiko put her first hand to the glass to stop him. Ryan stopped, then reached over to place his hand over hers. For a moment, they were one, and she smiled.

*　　*　　*　　*　　*

Hundreds of kilometers away, in the updraft over an atmospheric storm system, Cloud Dancer paused to absorb the image of her smile. It was warm and pleasant and filled him with a sense of hope. All at once, the Jovian felt an impulse to play.

Swiftly, gracefully, and with the perfect poise and composure of a ballerina, he soared back into the air. Cloud Dancer glided upward, then curved his body so he broke over the crest of some upper-level clouds, and did a vertical flip and hurled back towards the surface. Carried away by the simple joy in the moment, he continued dancing from cloud to cloud until the Space Station was far behind him, somewhere in the vast obscurity of the heavens, where the dawn rolled on into night.

Epilogue

In the months and years that followed . . . Mitchell Ryan was named as the official spokesman for the Jovians, and served as the leader of the independent Terran-Jovian colony for twenty years until his retirement. His youngest son Bill took over for him, while his oldest son Tom took the Baltimore Ravens to their fifth Superbowl championship in 2099. Doctor Yukiko Takahashi received the Nobel Peace Prize for her efforts to protect the Jovian lifeforms. Her son Hiroki grew up and became an astronaut.

Lloyd Cramden retired to write his memoirs, while Doctor Vasili Rudenko continued serving as the Chief Medical Officer until his retirement at ninety years of age. Lenny Provenzo's death inspired a cult following among science fiction fans, and to this day, they still await his second coming. Doctor Rachel Westin disappeared and was never heard from again.

Susan Ryan narrowly defeated her Democratic opponent in the 2092 Presidential Election, and became the third female President in the history of the United States. Her administration was fraught with scandal and corruption, and less than one year later, she was impeached and successfully removed from office. Two elementary schools, one in Canton, Ohio, and one in San Francisco, California, were named in honor of Scott Glenn and Hiroki Takahashi, respectively.

The Jovians were admitted to the United Planets as the first non-humans. They would not be the last.

About the Author

Dr. John L. Flynn is a three-time Hugo-nominated author and long-time science fiction fan and critic who has written seven books, numerous short stories, articles, reviews, and one screenplay. Born in Chicago, Illinois, on September 6, 1954, he has a Bachelor's and Master's Degree from the University of South Florida and a Ph.D. from Southern California University. He is a member of the Science Fiction Writers of America, and has been a regular contributor and columnist to dozens of science fiction magazines, including *Starlog, Not of This Earth, Sci-Fi Universe, Cinescape, Retrovision, Media History Digest, SFTV, SF Movieland, Monsterland, Enterprise, Nexxus, The Annapolis Review*, and *Collector's Corner*. In 1977, he received the M. Carolyn Parker award for outstanding journalism for his freelance work on several Florida daily newspapers, and in 1987, he was listed in *Who's Who Men of Achievement*. He sold his first book, *Future Threads*, in 1985. He has subsequently published five other books related to film, including *Cinematic Vampires, The Films of Arnold Schwarzenegger, Phantoms of the Opera, Dissecting Aliens,* and *War of the Worlds: From Wells* *to Spielberg*. Brickhouse Books published *Visions in Light and Shadow*, a collection of his literary short stories, in 2001. For the past three years, John has been nominated for the prestigious Hugo Award, which is the Science Fiction Achievement Award, for his science fiction writing. He has appeared on television (including the Sci-Fi Channel), spoken on the radio, and been a guest at national conferences because of his advocacy work in bringing the science fiction into the mainstream. In 1997, John switched gears to study Psychology, and earned a degree as a Clinical Psychologist. His study, "The Etiology of Sexual Addiction: Childhood Trauma as a Primary Determinant," has broken new ground in the diagnosis and treatment of sexual addiction. Today, Dr. Flynn is retired, living in Florida, and writes full-time. He has written 19 books all total.